Skylar

Kate Allenton

Discover other titles by Kate Allenton

At

www.kateallenton.com

ACKNOWLEDGMENTS

I'd like to acknowledge my
READERS....You all rock.
Thank you for taking a chance on my
books.

1 CHAPTER

"I'm not crazy," Skylar Love whispered to her best friend, Olivia Parks, while they strolled arm in arm down Main Street.

Their Sunday morning shopping ritual of treasure hunting, for great pieces to add to their little boutique, was something they both enjoyed. A few tourists trickled in and out of the island's souvenir shops. The strong summer breeze whipped through her brown hair, being held out of her face by sunglasses perched on top her head. The early morning sun promised a beautiful beach day for the vacationers. And beautiful beach day for vacationers meant empty shops and easier shopping for Sky and Olivia.

"Of course you're not," Olivia teased.

"I'm sure you find it normal to blow off Luke *Freakin'* Tanner. He's the hottest, most eligible bachelor to ever come out of our town."

Luke *Freakin'* Tanner was more than the hottest, most eligible bachelor. He was her first crush, and the only man whose presence made butterflies in her stomach do the limbo and dance the rumba. It sucked that his reason for asking her out had been a sham.

"It's a pity date, Olivia. Luke only asked as a favor to my brothers." Skylar shrugged off her disappointment. "He's in town this week visiting his mom. He'll be gone by next week."

"Sky, that's not pity I see in his eyes when he looks at you." Olivia sidestepped a young boy skateboarding on the sidewalk as they passed a shop they'd scavenged the weekend prior.

"He's probably horny and out to get laid," she teased. Not that she'd mind. A hot guy like him was probably used to being satisfied in work and play.

Olivia's eyes sparkled with mischief. "So, what if he is? You're not getting sex anywhere else. But if you take him for a test drive, I want all the juicy details."

"Now you're the one who's crazy."

Skylar had grown up with Luke. She'd watched as he built his fortune, amassing millions, and she'd seen the rail-thin models clinging on his arm in the tabloids. Luke was more than a great catch. He was a good guy, which was precisely why she'd said no. Falling for him was easy. She already had years ago. Offering her heart on a silver platter for him to crush was destined for disaster. *Nope, I'm not going there.*

"For some reason, my stupid brothers have it stuck in their heads that my breakup with Ryan destroyed me." Skylar rolled her eyes at the idea. "We both know I was the one who dumped his sorry ass."

"He rebounded fast. He's been spotted around town with Candy."

"She's after his money and clueless that he's broke. When she figures out he can't afford a manicure for her claws, she'll dump him too."

"It's a shame. He used to be a good guy, until he started drinking. If my brothers found out that he tried to hit me..." Skylar whistled and shook her head.

"Ryan is a cheater and a drunk. He made his bed and deserves whatever he gets." Olivia bumped Sky's shoulder. "I'm sure your brothers mean well by trying to help you move on."

Skylar walked into the thrift shop and let go of Olivia's arm as she strolled through the tight aisles, leaving the ugly memories behind her. She placed a smile

KATE ALLENTON

on her face, letting any thoughts of Ryan drift away. He wasn't ruining her day. Not anymore.

Tendrils and streams of different colored energy guided her toward the back of the store where she knew she'd find her next purchase. She'd been born with the gift of seeing energy in the air, similar to auras, but instead of them creating a circle, they were lines of color in her vision. As a child, she'd sit out on her tire swing and watch as the energies entwined with each other, giving her a spectacular show of lights and colors that only she could see. It wasn't until she'd started kindergarten that she realized others didn't see the same thing.

Skylar slowed beside Olivia, stopping in front of a rack, where Olivia was sifting through the hangers to get a better look. There was one thin, golden stream of light among the dull brown energy strands. "Besides, what do I have in common with Luke? I see ribbons of colors and half the town thinks I'm crazy."

Skylar gestured to the entire store as if Olivia could see what she'd meant.

"You know I can't see them," Olivia mumbled and kept looking through the rack. "And news flash, he's used to crazy. He is your brother's best friend. It's not like your gift is news to him."

Skylar shifted the dull brown strands

out of the way, pushing them to the side until the one golden strand remained. She followed the golden path from above the rack down to the hanger containing the perfect shirt. She pulled out the hanger and handed the vibrant purple silk blouse to her best friend. "This one."

"Oh, Sky, it's perfect." Olivia held the blouse higher toward the iridescent light, twirling the hanger between her fingers. The sparkle in her eyes matched her happiness because of the beautiful material. "You know, this is why I love shopping with you."

Sky nudged Olivia's arm. "And here I thought it was because you loved my personality, or even better, the after-shopping invite to Sunday lunch at my mom's house where you get to ogle my good-looking brothers."

Olivia grinned. "Eye candy sweetens the pot."

"Eww." Skylar moved farther into the store, coming to a stop in front of the jewelry counter. She squatted in front, her gaze roaming over all the prizes she'd be taking home.

"Can I help you find something, Skylar?" Maggie Montgomery, the owner of the thrift shop, asked from behind the counter.

"Can I get a closer look?" She gestured to the case.

Maggie opened the case, stepping out of Sky's way. "Have at it."

Skylar lifted her eyebrows in quick successions like a child that found a new favorite toy. Olivia grinned. Stepping around the case, Skylar made haste using her fingers to move the silver tendrils of energy out of the way until the gold ones remained. She followed the strands to their origins, lifting the intricate jewelry pieces out and placing them on the counter. The last box she pulled contained a pair of cufflinks. She grinned at the perfect pieces. An early birthday present for her brother's best friend. Hell, she'd grown up with Luke. He'd pulled her ponytail when she was young. He'd teased her when she'd come home with braces. Luke reminded her of a stray animal, always coming back for more after being fed. He was like family that never left. A date might be out of the question, but they were still friends.

She eased the box out with the cuff links, treating them as a treasure. They were antique. Beneath the dark blue stone, shimmers of color sparkled. They were unique and exquisite, just like Luke.

"Sky."

Skylar glanced up to find Olivia strumming her nails on the case.

"Did you hear a word I said?"

Skylar stood with the last box in her

hand. "Nope, sorry."

"You zoned out." She tapped the face of her watch. "We need to hurry, or your mom will stick us with dish duty."

Skylar moved out from around the counter, letting Maggie retake her place. "I'll take all of these, please."

"Excellent choices, Skylar. These pieces came in yesterday."

A couple hundred dollars and five minutes later, they were back in her car and heading to her mother's house.

"Are all your brothers showing up today?" Olivia twirled her hair when asking.

"I don't know." Skylar gave her a sideway glance. "If my mother has her way, they will."

Ten minutes later, Skylar parked behind her brother's big SUV among the other cars lining the road. "Your flirting choices are limited today." Skylar chuckled. "Only Flynn and Reed are here. Declan must be running late."

Olivia's smile dipped, and her shoulders deflated. What kind of best friend would Skylar be if she didn't know which brother Olivia was crushing on? They stepped out of the car.

"Have ya'll heard from Landon?" Olivia asked in a voice laced with concern.

"Not yet. Last we heard he was working on a super-secret mission."

Skylar worried about Landon. Out of her four brothers, Declan was the oldest and most pigheaded; Flynn was the jock; Reed was the nerd, and her baby brother, Landon, was, most times, the prankster out of the bunch. Each often barreled headfirst into danger, but Landon's quiet demeanor, when he'd been home last, had sent up red flags. The light in his eyes had unexplainably dimmed.

"I'm sure he's fine." Olivia linked their arms to pull Skylar from her thoughts.

Skylar's stomach rumbled as they walked up the sidewalk, getting closer to the smell of a Boston butt being cooked on the smoker in the backyard. The white smoke drifted above the house, perfuming and teasing the neighborhood with the delicious smells. She grinned and met Olivia's gaze.

"Barbeque," they announced at the same time.

"I hope she made her banana pudding."

Skylar unlatched the back gate and pulled it open, bypassing the front door into the house. "I'm sure she did, just for you."

Her mother's favorite old time melody filled the backyard, drifting to her ears and bringing back memories of her happy childhood. When Olivia and Skylar rounded the house, Skylar spotted her parents dancing on the patio to the music coming from the radio speakers.

"When I grow up, I hope my husband and I are just as in love as Mary and Martin."

"Who's the lucky guy, pipsqueak?" Flynn asked in passing. He spun around and walked backward giving them a big grin and a wink. "Don't answer that. I hope my name is still in the hat." He chuckled, spinning back around, not waiting for an answer.

"They tease you because they love you." Sky passed the pool, heading toward the patio. "They don't realize that one day you'll tease back."

"Today might just be that day."

"Something smells great," Sky called out while crossing the yard toward her parents.

"You sound surprised," her father joked.

"Absolutely not," Olivia chimed in and smiled as Martin threw his arm around them both, pulling them in close and kissing their foreheads. The greeting ritual occurred during every lunch or dinner they attended.

"Your father is the best grill master on the entire island; just ask any of the chefs at the hotel."

Martin released the girls and pulled Skylar's mom into his arms. Bending her backward he planted a kiss that would make newlyweds blush. No matter how often she'd seen him make that move, Skylar sighed and smiled each time.

"I might be the grill master, but she's the master of my heart." He winked.

"Oh, Martin." Her mom's eyes shined with love as she swatted Martin with the towel she had in her hands. Their personal energy when separate was beautiful by itself, but when joined, it turned into brilliant pink and white swirls. True love at its finest and the reason Skylar hadn't tied the knot...yet.

"Where's everyone?" Declan called from inside the house.

"We're in the back," Skylar answered, grabbing a chip from the bowl on the table and popping it into her mouth as she and Olivia sat in the weather-worn wicker chairs.

Declan stepped out on the patio, his dark hair styled with gel giving him the just woke up and rolled out of bed look. He gazed around the yard. Zeroing in on Olivia, he grinned. Her eyes narrowed in response. Well, well, well. Just what had Skylar missed? She leaned into Olivia.

"Something I should know?"

Olivia's cheeks flushed. Busted. Something had happened, and neither one of them had bothered to share.

Declan patted his dad on the back and

hugged his mother. "Luke's inside finishing up his call. He'll be out in a second," Declan explained to his mom while keeping Skylar pegged with his stare. She'd told her entire family that she and Ryan had broken up. She'd just left out the why and the fact that she'd been the one to kick him to the curb. If she had to guess, maybe the guys did think she was depressed.

"Wonderful," her mom answered. "I made his favorite chocolate cake for his birthday."

"Maybe it can help mend his broken heart." Declan raised a brow, still looking in Skylar's direction in challenge.

"Maybe the cake can be payment for your bribe to date me."

Her mother's breath hitched. "Declan Love, tell me you didn't."

"Oh, he did, Mom. And you know what...I think you should ground him," Skylar answered with a grin.

Olivia tossed her head back as her boisterous laughter filled the yard, making everyone else chuckle.

All laughing ceased the minute Luke stepped out on the patio in the process of rolling up his dress shirt sleeves. His royal blue energy swirling around him was lighter than normal, matching his stunning eyes. He lifted a brow sizing up the quieting group. "What'd I miss?"

"Declan's in trouble." Olivia linked her fingers together and rested them in her lap.

"I'm not surprised. What did he do?" Luke glanced around the group, waiting for an answer.

"Skylar thinks you asked her out because I forced you to do it," Declan answered, crossing his arms over his chest and pegging her with a stare.

"He didn't force me." Luke's brows dipped as he looked at Sky. "Quite the opposite. I told him I was going to ask you out, and he sucker-punched me."

Skylar's mouth parted. She had no comeback for his statement.

"You deserved it," Declan said in his own defense, the humor in his earlier tone turning serious. "She's always been off-limits. I'm not sure why you thought that changed."

"Off-limits?" Skylar barked. Her cheeks heated as she clenched her teeth. "Since when do you have a say in my personal life?"

"Since I'm your older brother, and you're a girl," he answered.

"I'll show you what this girl can do." Skylar went to push herself out of her chair when her mom whistled.

"Skylar." She shook her head before turning toward the cause of the ruckus. "Declan, you've done enough damage. You get dish duty." Her mother started barking out orders for everyone to help her in the kitchen, leaving Skylar and Luke alone on the patio.

The awkward silence between them grew. "Luke..."

He shoved his hands in his pockets and rocked on the balls of his feet. His lips twisted at the corners. "You underestimate our chemistry."

She rose, standing her ground. "I refuse to be just another flavor of the month. Forgive me if your ego can't take the hit."

"Ouch." He held his hand to his chest. "You think you've figured me out. You're not just a flavor, Sky." He closed the distance between them. With each step he took, her heartbeat quickened, but she kept her feet planted, refusing to believe his words. "I don't want just a taste. I want the whole damn dessert."

Her breath caught at the same time the group came back outside, ruining their moment. Luke retreated, stepping out of her personal space. Her mom carried the candle-lit cake over to the picnic table. "We're doing the birthday cake first in case Luke has to leave for his meeting."

"We should do dessert first all the time." Olivia grinned following behind with paper plates and forks while her dad and Declan pulled the meat from the smoker and disappeared back inside the house.

"Happy Birthday, Luke," Skylar said. "I really do wish you the best."

"If that were true, you'd let me take you out on one date. I'm not asking for the world, Sky. Just a single date that includes dinner and maybe a movie."

"Luke..."

"It's my birthday, Sky."

She rolled her eyes. "Fine, one date, and only because it's your birthday, but if you're hoping to get lucky, you'll be disappointed," she whispered as she sidestepped him and met the others over at the table where her mother started singing the traditional birthday song. Olivia joined in but couldn't keep the questioning look from her face. Declan and her dad joined the celebration.

"Mrs. Love, you didn't have to go to all of this trouble for me."

"It wasn't any trouble, Luke. You're part of the family." She glanced at Olivia. "Same as Olivia. You're both are always welcome in our home."

Declan glanced to his mother and then Olivia. A rosy pink color tinted her cheeks as they stared at each other. Feeling as if she'd been intruding on a special moment, Skylar looked away to find the birthday boy watching her, and unlike Olivia's blush, Skylar rolled her eyes and shook her head.

Luke leaned over the cake, closing his eyes. His lips moved in a silent wish before he blew out his candles. He gave Skylar a sideways glance and winked before her mother cut into the cake.

Flynn walked out of the house with two beers, handing one to Luke. "Congrats, old man. How old are you now? Fifty?"

"Thirty-two, and you're not that far behind me, Flynn."

Olivia handed Sky a plate with a slice of the chocolate cake.

"I left his present in the car." Sitting the cake on the table, Skylar headed back through the yard while the others were busy in conversation.

She opened the car, pulled out the box, and jogged back around to the gate, slowing when she found Luke casually leaning against the wood watching her.

"I thought you were making a break for it before we could set a time for dinner."

She grinned. "As if. I'm not scared of you." She handed him the box. "Happy Birthday."

He took the box, running his thumb over the lid. "Ah, Sky, you shouldn't have."

She gestured to the box before lacing her fingers to keep from fidgeting. "They reminded me of you."

The lines of his face softened while lifting the lid. A smile stretched over his lips. "I love them, they're beautiful." He met her gaze; his blue eyes sparkled, matching the energy floating around him. "I'll wear them every day."

He pressed a kissed to her cheek. "Thank you."

His lips were soft against her cheek and inches from her mouth. Too soon, he pulled away, leaving her with butterflies taking flight in her belly.

"It's time to eat," Declan announced, pulling her from her thoughts. He shook his head and disappeared into the backyard.

"He'll get used to it." Luke tossed his arm over her shoulders and didn't release her until they'd reached the French doors leading into the house. She pulled him to a stop.

"There's no need to bother trying to convince him." She straightened her shoulders. The truth remained. "You'll be gone soon and it won't matter."

"Dinner with me tonight at seven? You can pick the place, anywhere your heart desires."

She chewed her lip, debating her predicament. Agreeing to dinner was a mistake, but he didn't waste time making their plans concrete. She ran through the island's options in her mind, coming up with the only solution that worked. Somewhere safe, surrounded by others they knew that would keep her grounded. The hotel was the obvious choice. Her family owned and ran the damn thing. "You're staying at the hotel, right?"

"You're checking up on me?"

"My mother might have mentioned it." She smiled. "We'll eat at La Amour. I'll meet you there."

"You want to eat at the resort?" His lips twitched without her having to answer. "Of course you do. You know everyone there, and that way you can make sure I stay on my best behavior."

She chuckled. "You have a best behavior? I'm looking forward to seeing that."

"Fine," he agreed. "That means dressing for the occasion."

"I own other clothes besides jeans."

Skylar batted her eyes before walking into the house, trying hard to temper her newfound excitement. She slid into the seat next to her best friend, grabbing a French fry from her plate. Olivia nudged her beneath the table, her brow hitched.

"I'll fill you in later."

"Luke kissed her," Declan blabbered to the entire table.

Skylar's mouth parted, and she picked up a fry and tossed it at her brother. "On the cheek, you ass."

"Skylar, you weren't raised in a barn," her mother protested.

"She won't be able to do that tonight at La Amour. She'll get us kicked out of the restaurant."

Skylar flushed at the announcement. Didn't anyone believe in privacy anymore? Geesh.

"It won't be the first time," her mother announced. "When she was five, they made her eat in the kitchen with a drop cloth."

Laughter rounded the table.

"Mother." Skylar fixed a plate, ignoring their questioning looks and refusing to rehash the details of that story. No way in hell.

2 CHAPTER

Olivia helped Skylar carry their newly purchased items in through the back door of "Tidal Wave" and dropped them on the counter in the backroom with the rest of the merchandise that needed to be priced and tagged before it hit the sales floor. Sky's and Olivia's shop catered to more than just the tourists' needs, but to the locals as well. They both had a knack for spotting the cream of the crop in everything from clothes and fine crystal to fine jewelry. Skylar enjoyed the more vintage look and Olivia was more for the stylish modern day women.

"What are you going to wear on your date?" Olivia asked as they strolled out of the backroom and into the front part of the store.

"I have no idea." She let out a long sigh

and glanced around wondering if anything they had on hand might work.

"Skylar, Olivia. I wasn't expecting you." Michelle, the assistant store manager, announced as she approached. "Did you score us any new gems today?"

"Of course." Skylar answered noticing the few customers they had. "How's our traffic today?"

"Slow." Michelle folded her arms and glanced to the large front windows. "It's beautiful outside, so I'm thinking they're all at the beach. It'll pick up this afternoon; it always does."

The island was just off the East Coast of the United States. Anyone and everyone looking for a little vacation time without going far from home came to the island for a relaxing time. Without a huge port, they didn't have cruise ships that came; most of the time, everyone had to be ferried in, or if they owned a boat, they'd drive it over. The island was like a hidden oasis with five hotels, hot springs, the oceans and several caves that could be explored. Sky and her brothers were born on the island; they knew the tourists' schedules better than most.

The chime above the door sounded and Skylar grinned upon seeing her brother, Reed, as he waved before running his hand through his dark wavy hair. The five o'clock shadow and puffy blood shot eyes she'd noticed at lunch indicated he was neck deep in one of his computer projects. He was the brother that wouldn't know a good time if it smacked him on the ass, never leaving his house unless mandated by one of the family members, and even then, they'd have to pull him kicking and screaming from the computer.

"What's he doing here?" Olivia whispered.

"The only reason why he visits." Sky glanced at her best friend. "He needs a present and mom's birthday is coming up soon."

Reed stopped in front of them. "So, what did I get her this time?"

He asked and Sky chuckled. It was habit that all of her brothers assumed that she'd know the perfect gifts, no matter what the holiday; she was the go to person to pick the presents. She walked into the backroom and returned with a wrapped present. "You got her matching crystal earrings to the bracelet that Flynn is giving her."

Reed tossed his arm around Sky's shoulder. "You're the best."

"Funny how you and our brothers only remember that when it's convenient."

"I owe you." He answered ruffling her hair.

"And I'm collecting. We're expecting a shipment of various stuff and beach glass coming in from Blansett next month. I expect all of you to help."

"Wait, isn't Blansett known as the Salem of the south? What are they sending you? Spell books?"

"They happen to be a very prosperous beach town, and the store owners I'm dealing with have an exquisite eye for unique items. I doubt they'll be sending me spells."

"Okay, count me in. Just let me know what days and I'll help."

Reed left as quickly as he'd arrived.

"Back to what you're going to wear tonight?"

Skylar shrugged. "I'm sure I have something in my closet." She glanced at Olivia. "It's just a simple date; I'll figure it out."

"Yeah, just a simple date with Luke *freakin* Tanner."

****

Luke followed his assistant, Justin Healy, into the large, empty office building. "I still don't understand why you'd want to open another lab here. You'd be cutting yourself off from the rest of the world."

Love Island was a culture shock for any twenty-nine year old guy who grew up in New York. "It's time for a change," he answered, patting his friend on the back. "The economy on Love could use the boost from new money and new people."

"It's a mistake."

Luke shrugged. "A chance I'm willing to take." He walked farther into the building, glancing around at the unused offices. The bottom floor was perfect for human resources and the business offices. "Can we go upstairs?"

"It might be safer to take the stairs until we make sure the elevator is up to code."

Luke headed for the closest set of stairs and jogged up to the next level. Unlike the floor below, this space was wide and open and comprised of four outer brick walls.

"The owners had legal troubles and couldn't afford to finish this floor or the one above."

"What kind of legal troubles?" he asked, moving toward the floor-to-ceiling window. The dirt parking lot needed paving. He scanned the trees surrounding the building. Memories of fun camping trips slipped through his mind. He pushed the thought away. There was room to expand on the property.

"I'm not sure. The real estate agent suggested murder charges."

His gaze shot to Justin's. "Murder?"

Justin clasped his hands. "That's what

she said."

"I'll see what I can find out," he mumbled. He moved into the middle of the room and turned in a circle, taking in the promise the large space offered. "This floor is ideal for the labs. We can set it up how we want."

"What project are you going to work on here?"

"My personal projects."

"Well, we have one more building to see."

Luke checked the time and tapped his watch. He'd been looking at properties since finishing lunch with the Loves. "No need." He clapped his friend on the back. "This is it. Make it happen."

"Wait, why don't you at least check out the other property?"

He glanced over his shoulder as he opened the stairwell door. "I can't. I've got a date."

Justin gave a snide grin. "Leave it to you to find a date in less than forty-eight hours."

Luke chuckled, leaving Justin to follow him down the stairs. "This one's special."

"Sure she is. Just like the rest."

Luke shook his head. "None compare to her. Wish me luck."

Tonight had to be special if he had a shot at the happy life he'd been dreaming of. The women from the city didn't hold a candle to his Skylar. Not even close. It didn't matter what she had in her bank account or in her pedigree. His mind always drifted back to her. She was his, and now it was just a matter of getting her stubborn ass to agree. He was headed into uncharted waters, but he'd never backed down from a challenge, and he wouldn't start now. This date might be the most important night of his life. He had his work cut out for him. He dialed the concierge at the hotel. "Stanley, this is Mr. Tanner. Is everything set for tonight?"

"Yes, sir. We have your table reserved and the flowers you requested are waiting in your room. Did you need me to handle something else, sir?"

"No, thank you. I'll handle the rest. Thanks for your help."

"You're welcome, sir."

Luke hung up and called Declan. "Love."

"You working tonight?" Luke asked.

"Why? You getting butterflies for your date?"

"Screw you."

Declan chuckled. "Yeah, I'm at the office assigning officers their work zones. You'd be surprised how they fight like children over who gets the beach detail at the clubs during spring break."

"I'm surprised you're not handling that yourself."

"Bite me."

Luke chuckled. "Not working the beat was a sacrifice of taking the job of sheriff."

"Someone's got to do it. Might as well be me."

"There's no one better, my man. Listen, I need a favor."

"What's up?"

"I need the history on the Dagger building. I hear that the last owners were being held for murder or had legal issues."

"That's an understatement. One of the construction workers showed up for work one morning to find a dead guy, with two bullet holes to the chest, lying just inside the building."

"And you think the previous owners did it?"

"The gun was found hidden at their house, and they didn't have an alibi. To top it off, the man murdered was their accountant, and they were cooking the books. So regardless of the circumstantial evidence, they're still looking at doing time. They'd signed over ownership to their daughter, Megan Dagger, before the shit hit the fan and their property was seized."

"I'm thinking about setting up another lab."

The line went quiet. Luke had been planning on keeping the news below the radar until names were signed on the dotted line, but there was little he kept from his best friend.

"Is it because of Skylar?"

"Maybe. Look, it's not just because of Sky. It's a good business move too. I'm not thinking with my johnson."

"Dude, I don't want to hear about your johnson and my sister in the same sentence...ever."

Luke chuckled as he turned into the resort. "I've got to go get ready. How about hanging out tomorrow and watching the game?"

"My place?"

"Do you even have to ask? I'm homeless, remember?"

"You own at least five houses. You aren't homeless."

"On the island I am."

Declan chuckled. "Luke, don't forget this is my sister you're taking out tonight. She isn't one of your floozies from New York. If you hurt her..."

"If I hurt her, you can beat my ass until I'm black and blue. Enough said?"

"Yeah, enough said."

****

Sky slipped her fingers into the limo driver's hand and stepped out onto the sidewalk. When she'd said she'd meet him at the restaurant, this wasn't what she had in mind. But here she was, going on a date with a man scheduled to leave in one week's time. She slid her hand down her black ankle-length skirt before resting her hand on her stomach. She could do this. She'd eaten with Luke numerous times. She pulled at the hem on the matching top while questioning her choice of outfits. Her bed lay full of other discarded choices, from sexy dresses to casual pants. The two-piece skirt and top combo looked classy with a hint of sexy on the side.

The silky black and white material clung to her curves in all of the right places giving a glimpse of the prizes beneath, yet the length flowed to her feet with style and grace. Luke stood waiting in the lobby in a black business suit. He fidgeted with his Persian blue tie, pulling at the knot before straightening it again. The color matched not only his eyes, but the surrounding energy ribbons. She watched him through the glass front entrance, his nervous habits easy to spot. He turned his wrist, checking that the cufflinks were still in place. A smile split her lips. Luke looked up from the last fight with his tie and met her gaze. Her heart thumped wildly in her chest, and she silently wondered if he was nervous too.

"This is crazy," she whispered to herself as he stepped out of the sliding doors.

"It's too late to escape. You might as well eat," he said in jest as he approached and kissed her cheek. "You look beautiful."

Her cheeks heated in response. "Remind me why I agreed to this."

He held out his arm for her to take. "Because it's my birthday."

She wrapped her palm around his bicep. "Is that what you think?"

"Well, I was hoping it was because you wanted to spend time with me." He flashed a flirty smile, making her legs weak.

They walked into the five-star restaurant and were ushered to their table.

"Benjamin will be your server tonight. Enjoy," the woman said before leaving them to sit.

Luke pulled out her chair, waiting for her to sit before taking his own.

"Bonjour," Benjamin said in way of greeting until he spotted Skylar. "Hey Sky, you guys are a few minutes early."

"You can drop the charade; I know you're not French."

"Shh. Don't say that so loud." He put his finger to his lips, glancing at the other patrons to see who might have heard. "The customers don't know that. The bartender made you two of your favorites when he saw your name on the reservation list."

"Blue Hurricanes?" She smiled and

glanced at the bar. Her favorite bartender was serving a tourist. His unique energy was a dingy gray. She'd never seen another like it.

"Is that okay, Sky?" Luke asked.

She jerked her gaze back. "Of course, we'll start with those. Luke needs it to calm his nerves." She winked and grinned.

"They're waiting at the bar. I'll just go get them while you two decide on what to eat."

Benji was just handing them menus when a blonde woman in a designer black dress strolled by with extra emphasis on the swing of her hips.

"Thank you, Benjamin." Luke scanned the menu before laying it on the table.

"You can't possibly know what you want to eat."

"Are you kidding? Of course I do." He turned his gaze toward the kitchen. "Your father taught those guys to cook, and I know his specialty is anything grilled or smoked, so my obvious choice is the porterhouse steak."

She opened her menu and was debating her choices when the same blonde woman that had walked by before stopped at their table.

"Luke. What a pleasant surprise." Her voice was silky and laced with suggestion.

"Amanda," Luke answered with irritation. "What are you doing here?"

"I thought you'd be happy to see me."

"Stalking doesn't become you, Amanda."

Amanda's lips parted.

"There's nothing left to say." Luke placed his napkin on the table and rose.

"Because of her?" Amanda glared down her nose at Skylar. The puke yellow energy that surrounded her looked sick and dull. "She's not even in your class. You belong with someone like me."

"Skylar has more class in her little pinky than you'll ever have."

Amanda waved off his words. "When you come to your senses, I'm staying in suite 504."

Benjamin returned, carrying a serving tray with two glasses of blue liquor. Before Benjamin could place them on the table, Ryan, Skylar's ex-boyfriend, stumbled over to the table and careened into Amanda, knocking Benjamin off balance. The impact sent both glasses of drinks flying into Skylar's direction. Her fight-or-flight reflexes were stunned into slow motion. She tried to stand to get out of the way but wasn't quick enough. The liquid splashed, drenching Skylar's top.

"Oh, Sky." Luke grabbed his napkin and rounded the table.

"You stupid ass," Amanda growled at Ryan. His bloodshot eyes drifted unfocused around the room.

She'd expected chills from the cold liquid, but it had the opposite effect. The liquid wasn't cold on her chest. It was hot. She could hear the sizzling of her top. See the fibers disappearing right before her eyes. "Oh shit. It's burning through my top."

Benjamin reached for the glasses, and she screamed, "Don't touch them!"

She ran down the bathroom hallway. She rushed into the bathroom, flinging the top off and away from her body, not caring that she stood in her bra in front of the sink. Turning the faucet on, she leaned over, cupping the water into her hands and splashing it on her pink skin.

She ignored the other women in the bathroom, who gave her a wide berth, leaving the minute that her top flew across the room.

The water provided little relief as she hurried to cool her skin, not knowing if she was doing more damage than good. Her fingers shook beneath the stream as she splashed more water on her chest. The water slid down her stomach.

The door flew open and Skylar met Luke's gaze in the mirror.

"Are you okay?"

He hurried in, letting the door close behind him, a plastic bottle of honey in his hand.

"It burns." She bit back the tears that

formed in her eyes.

He turned her and flicked the lid open on the bottle of honey, squeezing the cold goo out onto his palm. "This will help."

He rubbed his palms together to smear the sticky stuff and placed his palms on her pink chest. The cold honey nipped the heat of whatever had been in her drink. She didn't care if it was gooey or if it took a week to get off her skin. She was happy for the reprieve.

"Where did you learn this?" she asked as he poured more into his hand to layer the stuff on thick.

"When you grow up on an island and work in a lab, it's good to know various remedies that work on burns. The honey will keep it from getting infected until we can get you to a hospital for proper treatment."

"What was in those drinks?"

"I'm not sure, but your father is going to be pissed. They've called your brother, and the restaurant manager has taken everyone else's drinks. It's starting to eat through the carpet. "

Her eyes widened. She glanced down at her soaked bra. "I can't walk out in just my bra, and there's no way in hell I'm putting that shirt back on."

"That's an easy fix, Sky," Luke answered, sliding his jacket off his arms and holding it open for her. "We'll go up to my room and get one of my shirts that you can wear to the ER."

"You realize, if I put that on, your jacket will never be the same."

He cleared his throat, his tone serious as he answered. "I don't give a damn about the jacket. I care about getting you the hell out of here."

She slid her arms through the coat and pulled it around her chest. The jacket was huge to fit his muscled frame. It dwarfed her in width and hung past her butt. With a hand on her elbow, he guided her out of the bathroom, only stopping in front of her brother and the other investigators that had arrived.

"Her top, with holes, is in the bathroom. Don't touch it with bare hands. It burned her skin."

Declan's worried gaze turned to her. "Let me see, Sky."

"Uh...no." She pursed her lips. "You can take my word for it. You need to figure out what the hell was in those drinks."

Luke led her away, but she glanced over her shoulder when he held open the door. "And...don't tell Mom."

He shook his head and pressed his lips into a fine line. "It's too late. Mom and dad already know and are on their way here. You can thank Benji for that. EMS is in the lobby waiting to treat you and decide if you need further treatment at the hospital."

"They can do it in my room," Luke called out, pulling her out the door and into the hotel. Two EMS technicians were standing in the lobby with their equipment in hand.

He pulled out his card key and handed it to Skylar. "Use my penthouse suite. It will give you some privacy. I'll be up in a few minutes. I need to talk to your brother."

"Thanks." She clutched the card key in her hand and stepped on the elevator. She held Luke's worried gaze until the doors slid closed.

****

Luke stormed back into the restaurant, bypassing the forensic teams swabbing for samples of the liquid.

Declan spotted him. "What the hell happened?"

Luke let out a shaky breath, surveying the surrounding chaos. "We hadn't even ordered yet. The waiter said that the bartender had drinks waiting for her. I'm not sure what he did with them before they were delivered. The waiter left us with menus while he went to get our drinks. Amanda stopped by our table, making a scene."

"What the hell was that psycho doing

here? Is she still stalking you?"

"I guess." Luke ran his hand through his hair. "She stopped and was creating a scene when the waiter returned. About that time, Skylar's ex-boyfriend, Ryan, stumbled into Amanda and Amanda into the waiter. There was a domino effect that ended with the drinks landing on Sky. She said it burned and ran to the bathroom. I didn't know what the hell was going on, just that I needed to find something to neutralize the burn. I raided the kitchen, found the honey, and used it to stop the burn from leaving permanent damage."

Declan crossed his arms over his chest. "Any idea who might have it in for either of you? You think it was coincidence Amanda and Ryan caused the accident?"

The forensic tech walked over to Declan. "It looks like drain cleaner, but I won't be sure until we get it back to the lab."

"Drain cleaner? Are you sure?" Declan asked the young woman.

"We were told they were Blue Hurricanes. Sky's usual drink," Luke added.

"If she's still walking, I can guarantee that's not her drink of choice. It's a good thing no one ingested this. There could have been permanent damage, and without medical help, she'd be dead."

"Thanks," Declan answered and waited for the woman to walk away. He pulled Luke out of earshot from the others. "What the hell is going on? You care to clue me in on who-in-the-hell is out to kill you?"

Luke rubbed his smooth-shaven skin. His special dinner had gone to shit. His initial response had been to grab Sky and get her the hell out of the building caveman-style if need be. He'd held his breath, trying to stop her burn. "No, but you can bet your ass we'll figure it out." He gave short, quick nods. "Call me when you're done and I'll let you know if we're still here or if we went to the hospital."

Luke clapped Declan on the back and left him to his investigating. Stabbing the button on the elevator, he waited while watching the numbers on the display as they counted down the floor numbers. His jaw ticked at the slow pace.

Stanley, the concierge, hurried to the elevator. His face pinched with concern. "Mr. Tanner. I'm so sorry. I hope Ms. Love is okay."

"You and me both," Luke grumbled as the elevator appeared and the door slid open.

"Call me directly if either of you need anything." He gave a sincere nod.

"Thanks, Stanley."

The door slid closed and Luke slumped

against the back wall while he replayed the evening's events. Amanda, Sky's ex, the waiter, hell, the bartender. Anyone could have spiked that drink, but he didn't understand why in the hell someone would want either of them dead. Luke ran his hands over his face, agitated that the night hadn't gone as planned. The elevator dinged; he stepped off and hurried down the hall and into his suite, passing the paramedics on the way out.

"How is she?"

"The spot will be tender and pink for a while, but she won't scar."

Thank god. He let out his first sigh of relief.

"She just needs to follow the instructions we gave her and continue to use the ointment every day until it's healed."

"Thank you." Luke shook their hands before walking into the room. He shut the door behind him and flicked the extra lock into place.

"Are you decent?" he called out, standing by the door.

She stepped around the corner, wearing one of his long-sleeved dress shirts. The buttons at the top lay open and were pushed away from her ointment-covered skin. She held one of the roses he'd forgotten to give her at dinner, lifting it to her nose and sniffing.

"They said I should air the burn spot as often as possible to help it heal."

He swallowed. He'd seen her in her bra, but seeing her in his shirt caused his shaft to jolt to life, pressing against the zipper of his pants. "I see you found your flowers."

She grinned. "I did. Thank you. I'm surprised you didn't take them to the restaurant."

"I was going to suggest a nightcap and give them to you then."

"And if I'd said no?"

He stepped farther into the living room and loosened his tie. "Then I would have had to give them to the maid."

She chuckled as he pulled his tie over his head, tossing it on the couch before flicking open the top button on his shirt. She was standing five feet away and he wanted to ravish her. It was nice to see her smile. Even better to know that she would be fine.

"You might have given her the wrong impression," she teased.

He stepped in front of her and eased the shirt material out of the way, trying his best not to expose her cleavage. If he'd had his way, she'd be topless right now. The angry pink marks were thickly covered in a greasy ointment slathered over her chest. His fingers traced the edge and he frowned.

"Your brother thinks someone is trying to kill us."

"What?"

"They think at least one, if not both drinks, was spiked with drain cleaner."

Her eyes widened in surprise. "Seriously?"

He nodded, caressing her arms. "Can you think of anyone that might want to harm you?"

"Not really. What about you?"

He figured that would be Sky's answer. She was so sweet and so giving that no one would have an angry thing to say about her, much less try to kill her. He, on the other hand, did.

"Several," he answered. The realization struck him hard, and he released his hold. His gaze traveled to the marks on her chest, and his heart clenched. "I've made lots of enemies in my line of work, and in my personal life. Hell, you met one tonight."

"Amanda?" she asked.

"Amanda is the one and only daughter of John McGregor, my number one competitor. She and I had dated."

"What happened?" She stepped toward him, and he turned his back to her and walked over to the window, lifting the curtain to stare down at the parking lot, avoiding her gaze.

"One day, I showed up at her work

unannounced, and I overheard her phone conversation. She repeatedly said 'I love you', to whom I don't know. She said to be patient, another month and she'd have me wrapped around her finger and her father would give her anything to dump me." He turned back to Sky. "Even reinstating her allowance and inheritance. Amanda laughed when she said she had it all planned out. She was going to get the ring and dump me at the altar. She was using me. I was nothing but a pawn in her game."

Skylar's eyes shined ripe with pity.

"I'm so sorry you got hurt." Skylar planted her balled fists on her hips. She looked ready to fight for his honor, and it was the cutest damn thing he'd ever seen.

His lips twitched. "Before I even heard the conversation, I'd planned to call things off."

"Why?"

"Because...she wasn't you. Sky, this was a mistake." He closed his eyes and pinched the bridge of his nose. "You should leave."

"What! Why?"

He walked over to the door and pulled it open. "Because I thought..."

"You thought what?"

He steeled himself to hold her gaze, refusing to look at the red marks on her chest. If he did, he'd tip his hand on why he was ready to let her go. He couldn't afford the chance she'd figure it out. "It doesn't matter what I thought. This won't work."

"So that's it?" she asked. "One lousy date and you're giving up?"

"Yes."

"I didn't peg you for a quitter, Luke."

His heart tightened. "I guess you don't really know me." He swallowed around the lump in his throat as she stormed into the bedroom, walking out with her shoes in her hands. If this was his fault, he had to shift the focus away from her. There was no way he'd let her get hurt. "I'll have the limo take you home."

"Don't bother. I can find my own way." She stopped in front of him and shoved the rose against his chest. "You don't deserve me, Luke."

He gripped the doorknob tightly in his hand to stop himself from reaching for her.

One last look into his eyes and she walked out without ever looking back.

He eased the door closed behind him. "I never did," he answered beneath his breath. The acknowledgement was a painful pill to swallow. His chest clenched. She was right. She deserved better, someone who wouldn't dare put her in the crossfire of someone trying to kill him.

3 CHAPTER

Skylar slammed her front door and flung her shoes across her living room. "Asshole," she grumbled to herself. Thankful she'd slipped out the back entrance, bypassing her brother and parents standing in the lobby, she'd caught a ride with Benji leaving after his shift.

She stormed to her room, pulling his shirt apart. Buttons flew in every direction, bouncing on her hardwood floors. She slid the offending material off her arms and tossed it on the floor, stomping on it for good measure because it belonged to that no-good, mind-changing man.

She didn't need this shit. She'd been the one to tell him it wasn't a good idea, but what did she do? She was stupid enough to listen to him because he was a nice guy, and now look where that had gotten her.

"Stupid jerk."

She walked into the bathroom and grabbed the porcelain sink, taking several deep, calming breaths. *We wouldn't have worked. It's better this way.* She lied to herself. Why did he do that to her? After repeatedly asking her out since he'd arrived home, she'd finally agreed to a date and he'd just let her leave. Who does that?

"That jackass bought me roses for cripes' sake."

She caught her angry gaze in the mirror, and her face softened as she stared at her reddened chest. She hadn't looked at it before, but now…under the bright bathroom lights, she understood more than what his words were telling her. The resignation in his eyes hadn't been from their crappy date. The shithead was pushing her away.

She tsked. "Stupid, stupid man."

She lifted her shoulders, giving her chest one last glance before getting in the bath to ease the tension in her muscles. Any other woman would give up at the first sign of rejection. It sucked for him;

she wasn't just any other woman. He needed help, even if he'd never ask for it from her. She took her time in the bath, careful of her minor burn, before climbing out. Her body relaxed as she redressed her chest in ointment and dressed in a loose top that wouldn't cling to her skin along with a pair of yoga pants. She'd gathered her hair and had put it in a ponytail when her doorbell rang.

"Sky...open up," Olivia called out.

Skylar opened the door to find her best friend pacing back and forth on her front porch. Her red cheeks glistened with perspiration; her damp hair was slicked back, and her jogging clothes were sticking to her as she caught her breath.

"Hey."

"Oh my god. I just heard. Are you okay?"

"I'm fine. Come on in." Sky spun on her heels and headed toward the kitchen to pour them both a glass of wine. She handed one to Olivia. "If you don't want wine, I can get you bottled water."

"No, I need this." She raised her glass in the air.

"Were you jogging?" Skylar asked in disbelief.

Olivia drank half her glass of wine before she answered. "It was a stupid idea, but never mind that. Why aren't you still with Luke?"

"He kicked me out," she answered. The realization still aggravated her. "Let's get back to what in the world possessed you to jog."

Olivia shrugged. Her cheeks reddened the longer Sky waited on an answer. "I figured it was time to get back in the game. I'm not getting any younger."

"I don't know why you torture yourself. You're beautiful just the way you are." Skylar grinned.

"Me neither." She plopped into one of the kitchen chairs and rubbed her calves. "Now, what do you mean he kicked you out? Is he an idiot? Did the smog from New York kill his brain cells?"

"Oh, he's still plenty smart. He's just been away so long he forgot that we Loves can see through his bullshit. I have to admit that I didn't catch on right away, but I understand now." She grinned.

"Now that sounds devious. You've got a plan, don't you?"

"I'm working on it. Let's just say that Luke Tanner has met his match."

"Now, do you care to tell me who tried to kill you?"

Skylar sipped her wine. "Probably his tramp ex-girlfriend that showed up, but I have no idea."

"Can't you use your mojo stuff with your superpowers and tap into the assassin."

Skylar chuckled. "You know I can't."

"I know." Olivia rose to her feet. "But it would be cool if you could. What about your brother's ability to spot liars? Maybe Declan should question everyone on the island."

"I'm sure he's already working on getting the names of witnesses and anyone who had access so he can round them up and quiz them to find the culprit."

"I guess that little gift comes in handy in his line of work."

"Yeah, I guess. It's a shame it doesn't hold up in a court of law."

Olivia walked back to the front door and pulled it open. "Let me know if you need any help being devious. I can do devious."

Skylar chuckled. Olivia didn't have a devious bone in her body. "Sure ya can. Will you schedule a few of the part-timers to cover at the shop the rest of the week?"

"Absolutely." Olivia walked out on the porch. "Call me if you need me." She wiggled her fingers and started in a light jog up the path.

Her usual emerald green energy streams had brightened to seafoam green. Either exercising was good for her, or it was from the mention of Declan. Skylar smiled, watching her friend cross the street and turn the corner out of sight.

****

Luke poured himself a glass of bourbon over rocks and collapsed into the plush living room chair. He rested his elbow on the armrest and sipped the burning liquid, letting it dull the reminder of how the night was supposed to have gone. He ran through the mental list of names that might have hated him enough to kill Sky or him. Amanda and her daddy held the first and second spot at the top of the list with a handful of other people he'd pissed off.

When he'd decided on pharmaceuticals as a career path, he hadn't accounted for how many people would have varying agendas. Everyone from the drug companies to the politicians and all the way to the insurance companies tried to manipulate him. Each liked their fingers in the pie, not to mention citizens that blamed him for deaths of loved ones for diseases he'd yet to cure. The world was filled with twisted people. When Luke had gone up against all of them with a cheaper version of a very expensive antibiotic, every roadblock possible had been thrown at him and his company, but he'd overcome the aversions and offered it on the market.

His company was one of the few for the people and not greedy about how much could be put in his pocket. It was his own little way of giving back to the world that had given him so much. His decision wasn't just the talk of the industry, but in the business field as well, each of them coming up with their own reasons on why he'd kept the drug so cheap. A marketing ploy for another product? The millions he'd make from people switching because of the price? Cheaper ingredients? Ridiculous accusations, each a stab in the dark into his character.

The average Joes of the world had called him a modern day Robin Hood. Taking from the rich and giving back to the poor. He liked to think he fell somewhere between. Compassion in that industry was hard to find. The people in his labs worked diligently to discover cures and help the needy. Compassion ran heavily through his veins. Had he started in a desk job, he might have turned out differently. He took another sip. Nope, even doing that, he knew he would have ended up just the same.

His life in the city was nothing more than smoke and mirrors. The women he dated no more than silicone looking to get a slice of him. His heart had always been on the island. He knew it even if he couldn't act on it. He'd lied to himself about it, but not anymore. The days of dating women like Amanda McGregor were over. He was ready for something more real, and he couldn't have that until he got rid of the cobwebs in his closet.

He set the drink on the table next to him and rose, running his hand through his hair. Drinking his sorrows away wouldn't help solve his problems. He would handle them like everything else in his life. Grabbing his card key off the table, he left. He stepped on the elevator and hit the number five on the panel. He might not own the damn place, but he sure as hell could make it known that Amanda wasn't welcome in his private world, the place he'd kept separate from his corporate life, not wanting to taint the people on the island. Her presence was a reminder of the dual lives he led; and right now, he wanted only to get back to the one person his soul craved. He wanted Skylar, and it was time for Amanda to quit playing her games.

The elevator dinged and Luke stepped off, heading toward room 504 and passing one of the night maids cleaning an empty room. He knocked on the door. A crashing sound came from inside.

"Open the door, Amanda. I know you're in there. I can hear you."

He waited for an answer, only to be met with silence. He beat his fist against the wood. The sound echoed through the hallway.

"You aren't going to get away with this. Open the damn door." He banged again.

The door next to Amanda's opened, and a man stuck his head out, wiping the sleep from his eyes. "Dude, some of us are trying to sleep."

Luke ignored him and knocked again. When she didn't answer, his head slumped forward in defeat. He took a deep calming breath; demanding she leave would have to wait. Just one more thing he'd tackle tomorrow.

He stepped back and made a quick apology to the neighbor before heading back down the hall. His mind raced with options on how best to handle her. The maid held towels pressed against her chest, giving him a wide berth as he passed.

"Sorry."

She nodded once in acknowledgement and continued to watch him until he stepped on the elevator. He hit the button for the penthouse and pinched the bridge of his nose. What the hell had he been thinking? That he could just leave everything behind? The elevator doors slid open and he stormed back into his suite, letting the door close behind him. Walking straight into the bedroom, he emptied his pockets before unbuttoning his shirt. He unhooked one of the cufflinks and set it on the dresser before reaching for the other. When he found the cufflink gone, he paused. His brows dipped as he searched the surrounding floor. Nothing. He retraced his steps to the living room, his gaze sweeping the carpeted area. Nothing.

"Great." He finished taking off the shirt and changing before returning to the living room. Grabbing a paper and a pen, he started a list of every single person he could think of that might have it in for him. From employees he'd terminated to competitors, even ex-girlfriends. He racked his brain, afraid he'd forgotten to add someone's name that thought he might have wronged them. Seven names rounded out his suspect list. Two women and the rest men. Three ex-employees that he'd fired, Amanda and her father, and two scientists that he'd just pulled his funding from, for lack of meeting deadlines or producing any viable results. No one but Justin knew why he'd come to visit, the trip disguised as a celebratory birthday visit, so he brushed any information of his new bid on the building to the side, as it was not even public knowledge yet. He was sure when word got out, he could add more to his list, locals that might look at a lab on the island as some hazardous health issue, but that was a worry for another day, not today.

Luke left the note on the table before taking a shower and heading to bed. The plans he'd mentally made to talk Sky into another date to wine and dine her were on hold. Finding the wannabe killer and stopping any additional attempts took priority.

4 CHAPTER

Skylar's stomach dipped and she clenched her fist when passing the closed sign hanging on the restaurant doors. Last night she hadn't considered any hotel or restaurant ramifications from what had happened, but the reminder was bold and in her face, and she was pissed. Crime scene tape was strung across the door. Anger seeped into her core as she pulled out her phone and shot off a text to her brother.

Any chance the attempt was to ruin the restaurant or the hotel?

Can't talk. I'll contact you in a few.

She shrugged and slid the phone back into her purse. Skylar quickened her pace through the hotel lobby, ignoring the stares and bypassing questions. Butterflies assaulted her belly, knowing in just mere minutes she'd be confronting Luke. She'd tried to mentally prepare herself for any of his retorts, but now that she was here, her stomach flipped and flopped as if the elevator was dropping from beneath her feet.

The elevator dinged the top floor, and she stepped out. "It's now or never."

She straightened her shoulders and lifted her chin as she rapped her knuckles against Luke's door.

"Just a sec," he called out. Locks unclicked before the door opened.

"Sky...What are you doing here?"

"Can I come in?"

He opened the door wider, letting her pass. "You shouldn't be here."

She fiddled with her car keys before spinning on her heels to meet his gaze. "You're an ass."

His lips twitched. "I thought that was evident. I'm sure your brother tried to warn you."

"No, see...that's the thing." She waved her keys around as she paced to the large hotel window. "You almost had me convinced to walk away." She turned to face him and her brow rose. "But you forgot something very important."

"Yeah, what's that?" he asked,

crossing his arms over his chest.

"We Loves...we don't leave our friends high and dry when they need us the most, no matter how stubborn and pigheaded they can get." She gave him a saucy grin and waited for his rebuttal.

He dropped his arms. The color of his eyes and energy darkened with his glare. "Sky, you don't understand how dangerous these people can be."

"Oh?" Her brow rose. "So you have it all figured out?" She pulled out her phone. "Tell me who, and I'll let Declan know so he can arrest them."

Luke let out an aggravated breath. "I don't know who it is yet, but I'm working on it."

"Great." She grinned. "Then we should be able to find this son of a bitch pretty quick."

"Sky—" His refusal was interrupted by a knock on the door. "This conversation isn't over yet."

"You're damn right it's not," she called after him.

Luke opened the door, and Declan stomped into the room, not waiting for an invitation. His gaze landed on Sky before turning and holding up a sealed evidence bag. "Do you care to tell me what the hell you were doing outside of room 504?"

"Wait, 504? That's Amanda's room." Skylar walked over to her brother and took the bag. The cufflink that she'd given Luke was sitting inside the plastic.

"Sky, it's not what you think."

She tried to hide the hurt in her eyes, and a knot grew in her stomach. "Did you go see her?"

"Yes," he answered without hesitation. "But it's not what you think. I went to tell her she's wasting her time here and I'd never take her back. I was going to insist that she leave, or I'd call her father to come get her."

"Did you talk to her?" Declan asked.

"No," Luke answered. "I banged on her door, but she never answered."

"Did she say anything to you?"

"No. I heard a crash inside, so I knew she was in there, but when her neighbor poked his head out into the hall and told me he was trying to sleep, I left."

"Can anyone else confirm your story?"

"Why?" Skylar turned to her brother.

"Luke, I need you to answer my question. Did anyone else see you banging on the door and when you walked away?"

"Yeah, one of the maids." He nodded. "She was restocking towels in one of the empty guest rooms. She watched me get on the elevator."

Declan let out a sigh. "I know you're telling the truth because of my abilities. We're still checking the security tapes to prove you weren't involved, but as a precaution, I'm going to need your alibi and I was hoping to avoid a trip to the station for questioning."

"What the hell do you mean, alibi?" Skylar handed the bag back to her brother.

"Amanda McGregor was found dead in her room this morning by one of the maids."

Skylar's breath hitched as she covered her mouth with her hand. Amanda was dead?

"What? How?" Luke asked.

"My forensic investigator, who was here last night, thinks she drank drain cleaner."

Skylar's eyes widened. "How can she tell?"

"Drain cleaner is some lethal shit. When ingested, it causes a whole slew of problems to the body. A few of those are bleeding from the eyes, nose, and ears. She was found lying on the floor with a glass near her hand. The bottle was sitting on the dresser. The room was in shambles and it looks like she put up a fight."

"Oh no," Skylar said.

Luke's eyes glassed over. He remained unmoving and quiet as if processing the news.

"Have you checked the security cameras to see if anyone was seen coming or leaving?" Sky asked. "Besides Mr.

Obvious," she said, gesturing to Luke.

"We've got a team acquiring everything."

"Luke, do you know anyone who would want her and you dead?"

Luke walked over to the table and picked up a piece of paper. He glanced at it once more before handing it to Declan. "I don't know about Amanda, but I made a list."

"Perfect." Declan ran his finger down the list of names. "I'll call in a favor and have the authorities on the mainland check alibis while we compare these names with the ferry's manifest to see who else might have followed you here. If the killer came in via personal boat or helicopter, that might be harder to track, but we'll check those angles too."

"Whoever is responsible knows where you're staying." Skylar added, walking into his room. She pulled clothes from his closet and shoved them into his bag.

"What are you doing?" Luke asked with Declan following him.

"You can't stay here. You're an open target."

"Sky, I'm going to be fine. I'll just be extra cautious."

"And what if somehow they get into the kitchen and they spike your food, or worse, they steal a waiter's uniform, come to deliver your food and shoot you."

"You watch way too much TV."

"Mmm hmm. Don't blame me if that psycho comes to kill you in your sleep. You watch. Someone is going to kidnap your ass, put you in handcuffs, weigh you down with concrete shoes, and dump your butt overboard into the ocean."

Declan and Luke smiled at each other.

"What? It could happen."

"Uh..." Declan cleared his throat. "What if the target isn't him and it's you, Sky?"

"What the hell do you mean the target could be Sky?" Luke asked while taking the shirts out of Skylar's hands and hanging them back up in the closet.

She tossed her hands in the air. "I'll be sleeping with my 9mm. I'm not sleeping with the damn fishies. When they come for me, they better be ten feet tall and bulletproof, or you won't be investigating a missing person but another homicide."

"Forensics found both glasses laced with the cleaner. If Amanda was trying to win you back, she wouldn't have tried to kill you." Declan shrugged. "What if it's Sky's enemy? This might not have anything to do with Luke."

"Why would it be Sky's enemy? She didn't even know Amanda."

Declan shrugged. "Technically, Amanda knocked the drink on Sky. For all we know, it could be a stalker and in some twisted sick sense, he may think that he was protecting Sky. We have no idea who we're dealing with yet."

Luke pulled the shirt back off the hanger and tossed it into the suitcase. He walked back to the closet and gathered the rest of his clothes, carrying them into the room and dumping them on the bed. The streams of color changed right before her eyes. His normal blue turned darker from determination. Declan glanced at her and winked.

A master manipulator at work. At least Declan knew what buttons to push to make Luke see the danger he was in, even if he had to twist the issue. She held in her smile.

"Don't worry. I'm not going to molest you," she teased and walked into the bathroom, helping him move along with packing his things.

"Honey, that's the last thing I'm worried about," he said from the bedroom.

She leaned around the doorway back into the bedroom. "Did you just call me honey?"

He grinned.

She walked out of the bathroom carrying his cologne while twisting the top back on tight. "You think this is funny?"

"Personally, I think you forgot to take your meds, Sky," Declan answered.

"She didn't forget her meds, Dec."

Luke moved to stand in front of her and rested his palms on her arms. "She's just worried, and this is how she handles it." He glanced over his shoulder at his best friend. "Remember when she was worried bed-wetter Tommy Sampson wasn't going to ask her to prom."

Skylar's mouth dropped open, and she brushed Luke's palms away from her. "And if you'll recall, I was right about that too." She narrowed her eyes. "Fine. Maybe I'm overreacting, but what if I'm not?" She glanced to her brother. "Someone has already tried to kill us once, and now Amanda's dead. Whoever killed Amanda, and spiked our drinks, isn't playing around."

She set the cologne on the dresser and walked out of the room into the living room. Plopping down on the couch, she cupped her head in her hands. Why was this happening? She clenched her eyes closed, replaying everything in her own life since Luke had arrived home. She'd broken up with Ryan, but he wasn't the type of guy to kill. She let out a deep breath, coming up short with any other suspects that might have been tied to her.

The couch dipped beside her and a hand rested on her back. Luke's intoxicating cologne drifted to her nose.

"How about this..." He rubbed small circles on her back. "All I have today are a few conference calls, and I can do those from anywhere. You and I can take the boat offshore where no one can find us while your brother figures everything out. That way we'll see anyone coming after us."

"Unless he's a long-range sniper. We wouldn't see him coming."

"You watch way too much crime TV. So how does a couple of days out on the water with me sound?"

Hope was restored that he wouldn't be leaving. She glanced up at him from beneath her lashes. "You'd do that for me?"

His face softened. "Of course." He rose and held out his hand. "I'll pack a small bag, leave my stuff here as a decoy, give your brother the key and then we'll swing by your house to get your things. We can be on the water by noon."

"You good with this?" she asked Declan and held her breath.

"Yep. We'll set it up with a tracking device, and as long as you two keep in contact if an emergency comes up, then we should be good."

"Or if you have another dead body," she mumbled and took Luke's hand. He let her pull him up from the couch. "We're going to need to stock the galley."

"We'll hit the grocery store on our way out," Luke called over his shoulder as he disappeared into his room.

Declan tossed his arm over Skylar's shoulder. "Take your 9mm, the Sig, and the flare gun. If you have any problems, don't hesitate to shoot."

She glanced up at him. "Thanks, Dec. Hopefully, it won't come to that."

Declan lifted the list of names in his hand. "I'll call you if we get a hit on his list."

"What if you don't? What then? We can't stay out on the water forever."

"We'll cross that bridge when we get to it." He gave her a reassuring squeeze.

"I hope you're right." She chewed her bottom lip and swallowed around her dry throat.

5 CHAPTER

The bright afternoon sun sparkled a prism of colors off the metal on the yacht's bow as it cruised through the water. Waves lapped against the boat as Luke stood behind the wheel, expertly steering the vessel toward an alcove he'd called the perfect hiding spot, which few locals knew existed. The streams of dark blue lightened the farther they got away from the dock. His shoulders eased as he idled into the spot. He cut the engine and dropped the anchor.

She didn't know a damn thing about boats, other than the ferry that carried them to the mainland.

He stepped back into the cabin and

rubbed his hands together. "What do you want to do first?"

She shrugged. "What are my options?"

He grinned. "Lie on deck and enjoy the sun, swim, fish? Whatever your little heart desires."

She didn't know about her heart, but her body was craving his touch. She'd stood beside him while he maneuvered the boat. His leg had pressed against hers and his hand had been planted on the small of her back. Since leaving the dock, he'd been constantly driving her need.

"How about relaxing in the sun? I think we could both use a breather."

He gestured to her shirt. "Not sure that's wise with your burn."

"I'll keep it covered and sit under the umbrella."

"Why don't you go below and change, and I'll get the refreshments."

She smiled and spun on her feet, heading to the room below where he'd stored their bags. The one bedroom and adjoining bath were small compared to what she was used to, but the boat provided all the comforts of home. Within minutes, she was dressed in her bikini, carrying her cover-up draped over her arm with a wide-brimmed hat and sunscreen in her hands. She found Luke on the deck securing the umbrella behind two chairs, where towels were spread out.

"That should work great."

He glanced up and rose from securing the umbrella. His mouth parted as his gaze drifted down her body to her toes and then back up, meeting her eyes. Her nipples pebbled in response. Her breasts felt heavy and full as she tried to calm her racing heart. The hunger in his eyes told her everything she needed to know. He wanted her as much as she wanted him. There was nothing he could say to deny his attraction. No words would suffice after the look in his eyes. He cleared his throat.

"This was a bad idea." He glanced down her body once more, visually caressing her with her eyes. "I should have taken you somewhere cold and off the island."

"Maybe," she teased. "But then I'd need your body heat to stay warm."

She walked to the chair and draped the cover-up over the back. After popping the top open on the sunscreen, she took her time lathering her legs, her belly, and parts of her chest where the pink was slowly fading. He stood still, watching every movement. She silently wondered if he was imagining that it was his hands on her skin everywhere she touched. He was about to find out. She held the tube out to him and turned.

"Do you mind?"

He squirted the sunscreen into his palm and lathered his hands together. He started on her shoulders and arms, in slow motion working the lotion into her skin. He stepped closer and whispered, "You're teasing me, Sky."

She playfully glanced over her shoulder when his fingers moved down her back. "I wouldn't have to if you'd make the first move." She grinned.

He dropped to his knees and smothered his hands in more lotion before he touched her ass. She moaned as he clenched and caressed the area, running his fingers down the line of her bathing suit, lifting the material to get beneath it. Her heart raced, and it took everything she had to stand still on her wobbly legs. When his fingers went between her thighs, she thought she'd die. He stopped before touching her aching core.

"Funny thing about teasing..." He slid his fingers free and rose behind her, pulling her back against his chest. His desire pressed hard on her back. He caressed her arms, his fingers teasing the outside of her breast. "It works both ways, baby," he whispered in her ear.

"Sky, it wasn't supposed to be like this. I wanted to date you, wine and dine you, show you that I'm the right man, the one you never knew you wanted. I wanted to be that for you. I didn't want you to be forced to spend time with me because of a killer."

"When have you ever known me to be forced into anything?" She turned in his embrace and ran her fingers up the contours of his chest and behind his neck. "You were right about our chemistry it's undeniable, Luke. Maybe it's time to see how far it takes us."

He held her gaze, his face unreadable.

"Sometimes you have to take a leap of faith into the unknown to get the greatest rewards. I'm ready to take that chance with you. Are you?"

His palms rested on her sides, and his hold slid lower with each of her confessions until they rested on her hips and stilled. His brows dipped. *Oh no you don't.* She stood on tippy toes and crushed her lips to his in a kiss meant to squash his doubts.

He tilted his head and opened for her. His tongue tasted and took as his hands grabbed her ass and pulled her closer. Her breasts pressed tightly against his chest. His racing heartbeat matched hers. He swallowed her moan.

Desire consumed her. They had on too many clothes. She wanted to feel him in ways she'd only dreamt of, to taste him on her lips.

He broke the kiss, his gaze intent. "Are you sure this is what you want?"

"Yes." The word had barely left her mouth before he lifted her by the ass. Her legs wound around his waist and he carried her below deck, kicking the door closed behind him.

He eased her onto the bed, slowly climbing up her body. He lay on his side, and his hand rested on her belly, the tips of his fingers sliding beneath her bikini bottom, where he left them.

"I've waited a long time for this." He looked up at her and held her gaze. "I can wait longer if you need me to."

"Shut up and make love to me, Luke."

His lips twisted into a grin. The ribbons of energy surrounding him turned a royal shade of blue as his fingers slid lower, beneath her suit. "You're awfully demanding."

"Are you surprised?" she answered.

"No." He slid his finger through her juices, teasing her without giving her what she wanted, what she needed. "You're nice and wet for me."

She opened her legs, giving him better access. "And ready."

He slipped a finger inside, and her eyes slid closed as he played, stroking the embers of her fire. He eased in two more, stretching her. He latched his teeth onto her bikini top and lowered it out of the way with his mouth. Sliding his teeth over her sensitive nipples, he moved to suck her flesh with his mouth.

She lifted her back off the bed, pushing farther into his mouth, and moaned. His fingers quickened as he rolled her nipple between his teeth, adding pressure. She lifted her hips off the bed, matching his thrusting fingers. She was close, so close.

"More." She moaned.

He pulled his fingers free and her eyes shot open.

He climbed to the end of the bed. "Don't worry, Sky. I'm just getting started. The first time you come for me, I want to be inside of you so you can clench around more than my fingers, baby."

He slid her bathing suit off and sat on his heels while running his fingers up her inner thighs as if admiring her. "You're so damn beautiful."

He slid off the bed and stepped out of his suit. He pulled on his cock as he held her gaze.

Her heart sped up as he climbed over her, lying on top of her. He slid his shaft through her juices before positioning it, and it took everything she had not to lift her hips so he'd slide inside.

He pressed tender kisses up the length of her neck before touching her lips.

He eased into her inch by solid inch until fully seated. "Damn, you're so tight, baby. I can feel you clenching me."

"If you don't start moving, I may have to hurt you."

He gave her a devious grin and eased out of her before thrusting back in, setting a pace that stole her breath.

"Next time longer." He panted as he buried his head in her shoulder and quickened the pace, making her toes curl. Her entire body coiled with need. She ran her fingers along his back, leaving a lover's mark. He groaned and lifted up, his shaft filling her and touching every nerve ending inside her body. She arched off the bed as her orgasm built to the point that she couldn't stop.

"Oh god." She moaned.

"Yeah, baby. Come with me."

Five more thrusts and she screamed his name as he sent her over the edge and her channel spasmed around him, pulling him with her. He seated himself fully and stilled, groaning as he filled her with his desire.

He remained on top of her as her heart slowed and she caught her breath. He pressed his lips to hers and held her gaze. His eyes sparkled in brilliant blue as he visually caressed her face. Their slick bodies remained joined. "I never knew..."

"That it could be that good?" she teased. "I had a feeling our first time would be explosive."

He rolled off her and pulled her into

the crook of his arm. "You've thought about this before, about us making love?"

"More times than I care to admit." She leaned up on her elbow and rested her head in her palm. "It's you I fantasize about when I'm using my toys."

His brow lifted. "You have toys?"

She smiled. "If you're good, I may have to show them to you."

"When all of this is over, I'm going to hold you to it." He kissed her once more and lifted to his elbows. "Until then, we should try to figure out who is trying to kill us."

He slid off the bed and went into the bathroom, returning with a warm, wet washcloth. He cleaned her and glanced up into her eyes. "We forgot protection."

"I'm clean. After Ryan cheated on me, I got tested, even though we always used protection, and don't worry, I'm on the pill. A girl can't be too careful."

"I've got a clean bill of health, too. After I overheard Amanda's conversation, I was checked."

He tossed the cloth into the hamper, slid his swim trunks back on, and handed her the bikini bottoms. "Why don't you get cleaned up; I'll fix us lunch and we'll go relax. Maybe between us, we can figure out who's doing this, and why so we can stop them."

He climbed over her body and kissed

her once more. "I'll never get enough of you."

She smiled and watched him leave, closing the door behind him.

"That just happened." She smiled, holding the bikini to her chest, waiting for the pitter-patter of her heart to slow.

Day turned into night without incident. They'd relaxed, talked, and ate, enjoying each other's company in a more relaxed way. The thought of him leaving at the end of the week was pushed to the back of her mind, and she tried as she might to ignore the heartache that was sure to follow. The lull of the water rocking the boat put them easily to sleep as she lay in his arms.

He'd woken her up with sweet kisses the next morning that progressed into making love. She'd never forget their first time, or any time after, clinging to the duration of the time they had left together.

After her shower, she found him on deck and took a minute to admire his shirtless body. He was looking out to sea.

"You aren't thinking of making a swim for it, are you?"

He chuckled. "No." He pointed to the darkening clouds farther out. "Hoping our luck holds out and that storm misses us."

She wrapped her arms around his waist and laid her head on his back, soaking in the warmth from his skin. "It's just another day in paradise."

He turned in her arms, resting his hands at her hips. "We have to go back today."

"What? Why?"

"Declan said McGregor checked into the hotel and he's looking for me."

"Luke, don't be stupid. You know that's not a good idea. That man is out for blood."

Luke ran his hand through his hair. "Sky...it's the right thing to do. I dated his daughter, and she's dead."

Sky stepped back out of his hold, crossing her arms over her chest. "And what if the killer spots us?"

He let out a lengthy sigh. "That's why you're staying on the boat."

"Like hell," she clipped out. "We're in this together, no matter what. You're not doing this without me. We're safer together, and you know it."

His energy signature deepened, and if she looked in a mirror, she knew that hers would match his strand for strand in intensity.

"The whole reason to come on the boat was to hide until the killer is caught. That's what Declan and you told me."

"That's not the only reason I need to go."

"We," she corrected.

"Declan has video of the killer leaving

her room five minutes after I left. He wants to see if we can ID him." He closed the distance between them and pulled her back into his arms. "We'll be careful." He kissed her forehead. "I won't let anything happen to you."

"It's not me I'm worried about," she murmured as she walked away. "I'll go change," she called out over her shoulder.

"I'm pulling anchor. Just come up when you're ready. Declan's going to meet us at the dock."

6 CHAPTER

A flicker of apprehension coursed through Luke as he stepped onto the pier. His eyes darted from boat to boat and person to person around the marina, looking for anyone who might look out of place or suspicious.

"Relax." Declan clapped him on the back. "We searched the pier and everyone on it while we were waiting on you. I have a team patrolling the perimeter and another one at the hotel. We've got McGregor set up in a conference room so your meeting won't take place in public."

Sky nudged her brother as she passed him. "I hope you checked him for deadly weapons."

Warmth spread through Luke's body. She really cared, even if her remarks didn't hold merit. She didn't hold back in her concern.

"Sky, the man is sixty-two years old."

She shrugged. "Just because he's older doesn't mean he can't shoot a gun."

"We'll check him before we get there," Declan said reassuringly. "We're taking you in through the service entrance straight to the room for less exposure."

The skies above them darkened in warning. She looked up, her face pinched as she climbed into the back seat of the SUV. Luke followed her gaze. "The storm's coming."

He clicked his seatbelt. "We'll be staying inland tonight."

Declan met Luke's gaze. He could read the worry in her brother's eyes. The same worry was playing havoc with his stomach. Dread filled his veins in the silence of the car. When they reached the service entrance, the door was being guarded by one of the deputies. He held it open as Declan escorted them through the hallway, passing the employees' break room and leading them into the conference hallway.

Declan entered first, asking McGregor to stand and hold out his arms. McGregor's glare never left Luke's as he was checked for weapons. "You can have a seat."

McGregor sat, and Luke took the chair across from him. "Stan, I'm sorry about Amanda. I can't imagine your grief."

"You should be, you little shit. You killed her."

"Mr. McGregor, Luke has been cleared in this case."

"Of course he has. You protect your kind on this poor excuse for an island."

"Sir...I'm the law on this island, and it would be in your best interest if you remembered that." Declan placed his hands on the table and met McGregor's gaze. "He's innocent, and I have video that proves it. Now, if you just wanted to come here so you can accuse him, then this meeting is over."

McGregor huffed and rose. "My daughter came here with him." He pointed an accusing finger at Luke.

"No, Stan, she didn't. I didn't even know she was here until we ran into her in the restaurant. Whatever she was doing was without my knowledge or my blessing. I broke things off with her months ago."

The lines on McGregor's face deepened. "She told me you proposed." He shook his head. "She had the ring to prove it."

"She was using me as a way to get you to give her back her inheritance. I overheard the entire conversation. When she was on the phone, she was joking with someone about how she had me wrapped around her finger and that it was only a matter of time before you'd give her back the money when she left me. Only I never gave her the chance. I called it off with her." Luke leaned back in his chair. "She might have had a ring, but I can guarantee you, it wasn't mine."

"Mr. McGregor, were you paying her bills? Do you have any idea who she could have been talking to?"

"I have no idea who she could have been talking to and I didn't pay her bills. Her spending habits were through the roof and I cut off her funds." He met Luke's gaze. "She did all of this over money?"

"I don't want to speculate. I can only tell you what I overheard, and it was a one-sided conversation."

"Do you have any idea who would want Amanda dead?" Declan steered the conversation back to the crime. "Any enemies or anything out of the ordinary that you've noticed recently?"

McGregor eased back into his seat and laced his fingers, resting his fist on his mouth as he stared at the table, lost in thought.

"No. I can't think of anyone." He glanced up at Declan. "What you have to understand was that she had a way of winning people over to seeing things her way. I can't think of anyone."

Declan pulled out his card and slid it across the table. "If you think of anything, call me. The ME will be calling you shortly to make arrangements for Amanda."

McGregor rose and picked up the card. "You are going to catch this son of bitch?"

Declan glanced back at Sky before he answered. "You can count on it."

Luke rounded the table and held out his hand. McGregor ignored it; Luke's attempt at a truce dismissed. It was a shame. If McGregor and Luke could ever see eye to eye, the world might have a few more miracles in store.

"I am sorry for your loss, Stan." Luke dropped his arm.

Luke turned to find Skylar silently waiting by the door, her eyes glassy. He opened the door and rested his hand on her lower back, escorting her out the same way they'd entered, back to the SUV. Declan followed behind them.

"He's telling the truth. He has no idea," Declan mumbled.

"Did you use your Jedi mind trick to figure that out, or did something else give it away?"

"No tricks, it's a natural occurrence. I just...know when they're lying, and he wasn't. He thinks his daughter was an angel."

It wasn't until they were back in the

SUV that Skylar spoke.

"That went better than I expected. That poor man." She buckled her belt. "His energy was a dull brown. He's in mourning."

Declan exchanged a few words with the cop at the door before sliding behind the wheel. He glanced up in the rearview mirror. "See, Sky, no one got hurt."

"I know." She grinned and pulled out her .45 from the back of her jeans. "I brought the heat. He wouldn't have stood a chance."

Both Declan and Luke turned in their seats.

"You came armed?" Luke asked, amazed that he hadn't noticed.

Declan turned back around with a chuckle. "Well...she is *my* sister."

****

Fifteen minutes later, they were seated in Declan's office. The TV monitor hanging on the wall was playing the recording from the hotel of the night Amanda died.

"Here you are." Declan pointed at the screen.

Sky paced behind where Luke was sitting. She stopped and watched as Luke banged on the door. "Where's the sound?"

"There isn't any," Declan answered without looking at her.

A few seconds later, Luke was leaving, and a couple minutes passed until Amanda's door opened.

Declan paused the video. "This is the guy. Keep watching. His hat is pulled to cover his face, not giving us a good shot on any of the cameras."

Luke stood as Declan pressed play again, and they watched as the man hurried down the hall and disappeared into the stairwell.

"Can you replay that?"

"Sure." Declan started the video over again and played it in slow motion.

He pointed to the screen as the man opened the stairwell door. "Stop."

Declan stopped the video.

"When he opens the door, it raises his jacket. You can see his gun."

"If he had a gun, why didn't he just shoot her? Why the horrible death?" Skylar asked.

"If I was profiling, it suggests that the kill wasn't random. He wanted her to suffer. We just have to figure out why." He glanced at Luke. "Do you know anyone that resembles him?"

"Just from his body build?" He rested his elbow on the arm crossed over his chest and stroked his five o'clock shadow. "No. The only person that came with me is my assistant, Justin Healy, and he's not even remotely that tall or big. What about a local or what if he's someone that has it in for Amanda?"

Skylar stepped closer to the screen and pointed to the paused picture. She glanced back at them while jabbing the picture. "His energy lines." She turned back to the screen and ran her fingers above the man. "They're black. I thought it was just the lighting in the hallway when he opened the door, but I should be able to see the light." She turned to them. "Do you guys see the light?"

"Yep, we see the light," Declan answered, crossing his arms over his chest. "You don't?"

"No, which means it's his energy I'm seeing." A smile split her lips as she spoke. "I should be able to identify him."

"Assuming he's the only one with black energy," Declan added.

"I've never seen another person with it on the island, Dec. Regardless of his face, I'll know him."

"Wait." Luke held up his hand. "From what I understand about your ability, the colors can lighten or darken depending on emotional state."

"For the most part," she answered. "Sometimes they can entwine with another person's when they've been together for a long time."

"Okay...so what if his color was black because he'd just killed her."

"Then, if he's not in the killing mood, the spectrum would be the same. My guess is he's medium to dark gray, depending on his mood, and black when he's furious."

"And have you seen anyone on the island with grey?"

She took the seat next to Luke and thought back to the restaurant incident. Her eyes widened and a smile split her lips. "I've seen grey. The guy was at the restaurant that night, sitting at the bar. I remember looking over at the bar after being told the bartender fixed our drinks and thinking his color was unique."

"Was he wearing a hat?" Declan asked.

She shook her head. "No. I'm positive he wasn't. He was dressed in one of those hideous flowered shirts."

Declan clapped his hands. "This fucker is going down." He rounded his desk and picked up the phone. "I need the surveillance brought in from the restaurant the night of the accident. Yes, I know you've already examined it. We have a new lead." He rolled his eyes as his tone deepened. "Just get it in here, now."

"Declan, this won't hold up in court. You're going to need more evidence."

"I'm working on it." Declan pulled out his chair and sat. "Right now, Sky is the only person who can ID him."

"Exactly!" Luke rose and moved to

stand behind Sky's chair. "She's the only person who can ID him. She doesn't need to be anywhere near this guy if we get a look at his face."

"What?" She glanced over her shoulder. "If I can help catch this guy just by walking around town, you better believe I'm going to do it." She turned in her chair. "It's the right thing to do." She threw the same words he'd used on her back at him. "Who's next? You, your parents, mine?" She stood. "Listen." She took a deep breath knowing she must use reason with Luke. "I'm not going to engage him if I find him. I'm not stupid."

"No, stupid is you walking through town as an open target. What if this guy has already left the island?"

"There's one way to find out." Declan glanced at her. "You'll have to review ferry footage of the passengers boarding. Are you up for that?"

She nodded. She'd do anything to catch this guy, even if it meant watching hours of boring footage of people leaving the island.

"Great, after we review the restaurant tape and have a positive ID, I'll have somewhere to start looking while you guys stay at the family cabin near the waterfall and review the film." He glanced at Luke. "She's safe with you and out of the way. Acceptable?"

"Shouldn't you be asking me?" she interrupted.

"No," they both answered.

"That answer will get both of you hurt."

"That's a good plan." Luke ignored her glare. "We'll be twenty minutes outside of town and close enough to get back in an emergency." He pulled out his phone and dialed numbers. "I just need to call Justin and tell him I'm out of commission for a few days and to reschedule my appointments."

Luke moved over by the window and was talking on the phone when a deputy walked in with a disk in his hand. Declan popped out the security footage and slid the disk into the slot. The screen popped to life and he paused the video until Luke finished his conversation.

Luke's brows were drawn together, the fine lines between them deep.

"What's wrong?" she asked.

"Nothing. I'm just having a hard time closing a deal. You can play the tape."

Declan used the remote, and the video played on the screen. Dec fast-forwarded until closer to their date and then resumed the feed. "Let me know when you see him."

She pointed toward the end of the bar. "He was sitting here."

Moments later, a man sat on the stool.

The same man she'd seen that night. "That's him."

Declan took the feed frame by frame until he had a good shot of the guy's face and paused it. Judging by the looks of him, he was a tall guy, big framed with a dark tan that might indicate he could be local. He had a small mustache on his face with high cheekbones. He glanced at Luke. "Do you recognize him?"

"No." He shook his head.

"Why would a complete stranger try to kill us? I don't get it." Sky rose and paced the room. "This doesn't make any sense. Even assuming he was working for Amanda, and she had it out for you, why did he kill her?"

"We don't know he was working for her, but maybe she promised him money and didn't pay him when we both survived. Money is a reason to kill," Declan was quick to say. "But we'll know soon enough after we find him. This island isn't big enough for him to just disappear. I'll contact all of the hotels and pass his picture around and start looking through each of their lobby security feeds. Maybe we can trace his steps"

"That's assuming he's still here," Luke added.

"Only one way to find out. We'll know more once you review the ferry footage, but in the meantime, I'm going to put out an APB on this bastard and start searching for him. He doesn't know this island. There are only so many places he can be staying."

7 CHAPTER

After getting settled in the cabin and eating a light lunch, Skylar popped in the first surveillance security disk from the ferry. She relaxed on the couch and propped her feet on Luke's lap as they watched the tourists coming and going from the boat, both searching the crowds for the killer. His fingers dug into her soles, releasing the tension she hadn't realized she'd been carrying.

"You know, I can think of several other things we could be doing."

His hand slowly crept up her thigh and she swatted at him. "Work first, play time later."

"You're right." He lifted her feet and

slid off the couch to sit on the floor. "There's plenty of time for that later."

Plenty of time? "Luke, when are you scheduled to go back?"

Luke shrugged. "When I'm ready. I mean I have to go back and get some things handled, but..." He paused the DVD and turned to look at her. "I'm buying a building here on the island and opening one of my labs. It'll be my home base."

Words escaped her. "Come again?"

He laid his hand on her leg. "I'm moving home, Sky. This is where I belong."

She sat up on the couch, and butterflies danced in her stomach. "I don't understand. I thought you liked New York and big-city living. Why would you do that? Please don't say that you're doing it to be near me."

Luke rose. "What if I was? What would be so terribly wrong with that idea? After last night, I thought it was settled, that we'd see where this relationship took us. I'm an all-in kind of guy, Sky."

"Luke, you have a life outside of the island. What if we don't work out? Are you going to uproot your employees again and leave?"

He sat on the couch beside her. "You're breaking us up before we even get off the ground, Sky. Don't you think you're jumping the gun?"

"Me!" She scooted him out of the way and moved to the middle of the living room. "I'm not the one jumping the gun and buying a freakin' building."

He shrugged. "The building is a sound investment for my research, and I'll be closer to my parents and my best friend, not to mention you."

She crossed her arms over her chest. "Who else knows about this? Does Declan know?"

"Of course he does. I had to ask him about the Dagger Building and what they were involved in. Other than him, only my assistant, Justin, knows."

She turned and let out a sigh. "All of your employees..."

"Those people will be just fine." He rose and moved behind her, wrapping his arms around her waist. "I'm keeping the other building, and they'll have a choice before I bring in help from outside the company. No one is going to lose their job." He pressed a kiss to her neck. "And as for us, sure I want us to work out, and I'm thinking one day we could have a future, but I'm willing to wait until we're on the same page. I'm not proposing, Skylar. I'm making a move back to the town where I grew up." He turned her in his arms. "You're a bonus."

Skylar chewed her bottom lip. Her heart thumped against her ribs as she replayed his words. He was moving here. He was moving back. Her lips formed into a smile, and she watched his eyes twinkle with light. "Okay." She nodded. "I know it's your choice. I just don't want you regretting it."

"I won't," he was quick to assure her before laying a kiss on her lips. He turned her and smacked her on the ass. "Now, let's get back to work. The sooner we're done, the faster I can take you to bed."

With almost forty-eight hours of video to review, she got comfortable on the couch and hit the play button, trying to analyze every person that came and went. Four hours later, she rubbed her tired eyes and hit Pause, glancing over her shoulder to watch Luke washing dishes.

"Sorry I didn't help."

"You are helping." He glanced back at her. "You've got the boring job of looking for a needle in a haystack. "I guess since you're not screaming, you haven't had any luck yet?"

She rested her arms on the back of the couch. "No and all the colors are making my eyes cross."

Luke turned off the spigot and dried his hands on a towel. "Maybe you should take a break. It looks like the storm is taking it's time arriving. How about a walk?"

She checked the time. "It's almost

eight."

Skylar's cell phone rang and their gazes darted across the room.

"Who would be calling you?"

She shrugged and stood. "I don't know. Olivia's manning the store. Maybe she's having a problem."

She answered, "Hello?"

"Ms. Love?" She could barely hear the man through the distinct sound of sirens wailing in the background.

"Yes?"

"This is Fire Chief Buchannan. We need you to come down to your shop."

Her heart raced at his words. "Is everyone okay?"

"There was a casualty, but not from the fire, ma'am. I'll explain when you get here."

Oh god. "Yes, of course. I'll be right there."

She shoved the phone into her pocket and manically searched the table for Luke's keys.

"What's wrong?"

She shook her head and he took her hands.

"Sky, talk to me."

"There's been a fire. Someone was hurt. I have to go."

He nodded. "Okay, let's go."

"I need the keys."

He pulled them out of his pocket and

dangled them in front of her. "I'm driving. You can call Declan and Olivia on the way."

Her feet tapped on the passenger floor mat as Olivia's phone went to voice mail for the second time. "She's still not answering."

"Maybe she's talking to the fire guys."

She punched in Declan's number. He answered on the first ring. "I just heard. Where are you?"

"We're five minutes away. Are you there? How bad is it?"

"I'm just pulling up. Oh, Sky...."

"What?"

"Fire is shooting from the roof."

Skylar closed her eyes and lowered her head. Tears welled behind her eyes. "They said there was a casualty."

"I'm walking up to the ambulance now. Hang tight..."

What seemed like an eternity passed while she waited for Declan to tell her who was hurt. "Sky." His voice lowered, and anger seeped from the edges. "It's Olivia. She's got blunt force trauma to the back of the head, and they're taking her to the hospital. I'm going with them, and when you're done with the fire department, meet me there."

Her forming tears slipped free. "Don't leave her, Declan. Do you hear me? I'll be there as soon as I can, but you don't leave her side. Promise me."

"Sky, I won't leave her. I promise."

She hit End and rested the phone in her lap. Luke entwined his fingers through Sky's. "What did he say?"

"Olivia has blunt force trauma. He's going with her to the hospital. We have to deal with the fire before I can get to her."

He squeezed her fingers. "He'll keep us posted." She tried to give him a reassuring smile and failed miserably.

"If anything happens to her..."

"Olivia is in good hands. Dec will protect her with his life. You and I both know that."

She took a deep breath and wiped her tear-stained face. "You're right. I know you are. We can handle this."

He pressed his lips to her hand. "Of course we can, baby."

Skylar turned her gaze to the window, the passing beauty of the island tainted by what unimaginable scene might lie ahead. Olivia in the hospital and their shared store potentially in ruins. Her gut clenched as she swallowed around the lump in her throat. The killer and his trail of destruction would haunt her memories for years to come.

"Oh my god." She pointed to the smoke billowing over the tops of the trees as lightning flashed across the angry sky, the storm slowly making its way toward the island. The old legends believed it to be an impending omen, but she disagreed. The water was a blessing to her, a source of nutrients for their green vegetation to thrive. Only time would tell if the rain did more damage than good concerning the fire looming in the distance.

Luke turned on Pike Drive and slowed as he approached the chaotic scene. Fireman swept water, spraying from the hose, back and forth across the rooftop of the two-story building as others scurried around the street. Bile rose to her throat, clogging her words. One of her most dreaded fears was realized. Townspeople and bystanders stood at a safe distance, watching as her life fell into ruins. Luke parked and they both got out. She stood motionless by the door, watching the destruction of her life's work as the fire licked the night sky.

Luke appeared by her side, putting a reassuring hand on her back. "You'll rebuild."

She turned to look at him, biting back the tears. She nodded as he led her toward the young fire chief, Cole Buchannan.

"Chief," she called out, sidestepping over the hose running along the ground. "I'm Skylar Love."

Cole glanced up from his clipboard and met her halfway. "Ms. Love." He turned toward the building. "As you can see, you're looking at a total loss." He turned back to her, ignoring the horrendous scene behind him. "It's still too soon to speculate, but we believe it was arson. A witness saw a man running from the back entrance after hearing a woman's scream."

"My business partner, Olivia Parks," she answered, unable to take her eyes off the carnage of everything she'd spent her life building. "You say there was a witness?"

"Yeah, he's the one that called the cops and carried Olivia to safety when he noticed the fire inside the building. Right now we're just trying to contain the blaze. We'll be here for hours making sure that it's out. We haven't found anyone else. Do you know if anyone was working?"

She shook her head. "There shouldn't have been. My partner and I do the closings at night after we send the staff home."

Luke wrapped his arm around her waist in support.

"Chief, I appreciate everything you're doing, but we've got to go to the hospital to check on Olivia. Is that all you needed?"

"I understand." Cole unclipped a card from his clipboard and handed it to her. "The fire inspector will call you with his findings, and we'll keep you apprised of the situation."

"Thank you." Luke shook the chief's hand before leading Skylar away. She glanced at the black charred brick on the building one last time as she climbed into the SUV.

Luke climbed in the other side and buckled his belt but didn't move to start the ignition as he quietly observed the scene. "Sky, I think we should leave the island."

"What? No," she answered without hesitation. "This asshole is not running me out of my damn town." She spoke her words through gritted teeth. "The only thing this shithead has done is piss me the fuck off."

"Sky...we don't even know that it was him."

Sky rested her head against the seat and inhaled a deep, calming breath to combat the raging nerves running through her body.

"Don't we?" She glanced at him. "Who else could have done it?"

"I don't know." He started the ignition and did a U-turn toward the hospital.

8 CHAPTER

Luke pulled up to the front of the hospital ER and stopped. "Go ahead. Go find her. I'm just going to park."

She pulled the handle on the door, only stopping when he placed his hand over hers. "Sky...this guy is still on the loose. Be careful."

"I will." She leaned over and gave him a quick kiss before sliding out. She headed inside the building. The ER was quiet. She passed the few patients waiting and approached the check-in desk. "I'm here to see Olivia Parks."

"I'm sorry, miss. I have strict orders that all of her visitors have to be cleared by the police."

Sky pressed her lips together. She'd asked for this, protection for Olivia, and it wasn't the damn nurse's fault she was following orders. "Tell Declan Love that his sister is here, and if he doesn't let me back this minute, that I'm going to make a scene."

The nurse's lips twitched. "Yes, ma'am."

She quickly picked up the phone and lowered her voice as she talked. Seconds later, after hanging up, she gestured to the door. "You can go back. Exam Room 3."

"Luke Tanner is behind me. He's also allowed," she informed the woman.

The nurse gestured to the locked door and pushed a button, turning the light green.

"Thank you," Sky called over her shoulder while opening the door and quickening her steps through the hall. She didn't have to read the door numbers to know which one was Olivia's room. A cop stood guard in front.

"Skylar." He gave her a quick nod and stepped aside.

"Luke Tanner is parking the car. Let him in when he arrives."

He gave her a quick nod before she walked inside the room.

Olivia lay on the bed, her angry eyes narrowed at Declan as he stood next to the bed, with a smile on his face.

"Am I interrupting?"

"Tell your brother I'm not staying with him."

Skylar's gaze darted to Declan. "Sorry, Olivia, I agree with Declan. Under the circumstances, it's best that you do stay with him."

"Unbelievable." She hit her hands against the mattress. "My own best friend isn't on my side."

"Oh, honey." Skylar moved to sit on the bed next to Olivia. "There's a killer on the loose. He's tried to kill Luke and me, and now he's burned down our shop and hurt you. I just want you to be safe. Will you do this for me?" Sky pushed out her bottom lip and batted her eyelashes.

"Seriously, the pout face?"

Skylar grinned. "Whatever it takes."

"Fine." Olivia sat up farther on the bed. "Now tell me about the damage."

"Total loss," Luke answered, walking in the door.

"No." Olivia gasped, her gaze darting to Skylar for confirmation. "Tell me he's lying."

"Afraid not." Skylar rested her hand over Olivia's. "But just think. We wanted to remodel. Now we'll just have to redo the building to go with it."

"When I suggested remodeling, this isn't exactly what I meant."

"I know." Skylar gave Olivia a sad

smile. "The shop closed at six tonight. What were you doing there so late?"

"I wasn't," she answered. "I'd already left and was halfway home when I realized I had forgotten the bank bag, so I went back. I unlocked the back door, walked in, and struggled to get my key out. I saw the guy out of the corner of my eye and screamed. That was the last thing I remember."

"You think she interrupted him?" She turned a worried gaze at her brother.

"It's possible."

She glanced over her shoulder at Luke. His brows furrowed as he rubbed his chin. "The guy who called the police said that he heard her scream, and saw the man run. He must have been leaving after starting the fire."

She pushed all thoughts of the man ruining her life out of her mind and returned her gaze to Olivia. "How are you? Have you seen the doctor yet?"

"Yes," Declan answered. "She's got a slight concussion and he wants to keep her overnight for observation."

"I can answer my own questions," Olivia snapped.

Declan's brow rose, but he remained silent.

"I should be released tomorrow."

"Dec, are you staying with her, or are you posting guards?"

"I'm staying."

"No, you're not. I don't need you here." Olivia huffed.

"Olivia. You need someone with you," Sky calmly reminded her.

"Then you stay with me, Sky."

"You know, that's not a bad idea," Declan answered.

"What?" Luke protested. "Are you nuts?"

Declan nodded toward the door. "Come on, Luke. Let's go get some coffee and give the girls a few minutes alone."

****

Luke followed Declan out of the room, clenching his fists at his sides. "What the hell are you thinking?" he demanded as they neared the waiting room.

"I'm thinking this is our only break to catch this creep."

"I don't know what plan you have rolling around in your head, but you are NOT using them as bait."

Declan poured two cups of coffee, handing one to Luke. Declan poured sugar in his. "Let's face the facts. If this guy even remotely thinks Olivia can ID him, then he'll be gunning for her. My guess is he shows up here to finish the job before she can give the police a sketch."

"And you think them staying here is

good, why?" Luke asked before sipping his black coffee, letting the liquid warm his throat.

"That's easy. We'll set the trap. When he shows up, bam, we got him."

Luke rubbed his neck. "And just how are you planning to do that?"

"We'll act like Olivia and Skylar are getting settled in their room, and we'll move them into the next room through an adjoining door with a guard posted inside the room. If the killer thinks that Olivia and Sky are easy to access, he'll jump at the chance to kill two birds with one stone."

"And you're going to be waiting for him?"

"I'll call in the detail and make sure the place is covered. They'll dress undercover as doctors or whatever. I'll be waiting in the room, and you can watch from the security office. When you see him on the monitors, you can alert us he's on his way. I'll also pass out his picture to the rest of the security staff."

"And if he doesn't show?"

"Then Olivia is placed under guard until the threat is neutralized, and Sky and you go back into hiding." Declan clapped Luke's shoulder. "Listen, we know what this asshole looks like now. When we catch him, and we will catch him, we'll get the answers, even if I have to beat them out of him."

Luke's cell rang and he was quick to answer. "Tanner."

"I'm at the hotel. Where are you? We need to talk," Justin said in a worried tone.

"I'm at the hospital. What's up?"

"I need you to come back to the hotel. I have an update on the building."

"I can't leave...."

"Yes, you can," Declan said.

"Hang on a sec." Luke covered the phone with his hand.

"You need to leave so the guy thinks the girls are alone. I'll get you a doctor's pass, and you can park in the garage when you get back. Slip in through the side door and go straight to the security office."

Luke let out an exasperated breath and uncovered the phone. "I'll be there in fifteen minutes. Meet me in the bar." He disconnected the call and shoved the phone into his pocket. "Declan, I'm counting on you to keep her safe."

"Dude, she's my sister. My mom would kill me if I let anything happen to her."

"Are you going to tell them your plan?"

"Are you crazy? The less they know the better."

"I hope you know what you're doing." Luke tossed his coffee in the garbage. "Tell Skylar I had to run to the hotel. If I go back in there and tell her, she'll protest to come with me."

"She'd kick my ass if I let you go alone. I'll send one of the guards with you, just in case."

"Fine. Tell her I'll be back as soon as I can."

****

Luke bustled into the hotel lobby and straight to the bar, where Justin was waiting at a table in the back, sipping a Crown and Coke, his drink of choice. He waved a folder in the air.

Luke sat where he could keep his eye on the cop waiting outside and anyone who might come up behind him.

"What's with the cop?"

"Long story. Too long to get into right now. What was so important?" Luke asked, leaning back in his chair, trying to act relaxed when that was the complete opposite of how he felt. Trepidation had churned in his gut when leaving the hospital, leaving Sky for the first time since everything started. He glanced back out front, trying to recall if the security tape was still around the restaurant next door. A sobering reality; their hell had all started here.

Justin slid the file over to him. "I have the appraisal on the Dagger building and the information on the owner. It's the Dagger's daughter. They were probably tipped off by the local cops that they were going to get arrested and started transferring assets."

Luke kept his gaze down as he flipped through the file. "Careful what you say about the locals; I'm one of them and I know for a fact this town isn't run that way."

Justin's hands shot up in the air. "No offense, Luke."

He flipped past the parents to the appraisal and flipped to the last page where the total was. Satisfied, he shut the file and slid it back. "Give her the asking price." He rose and turned to walk away.

"You don't even want to negotiate?"

He slowly turned back to Justin. "I want this done, and I want to be moving in staff and furniture within the month."

Justin picked up the file and nodded. "I'll make the call and get them to push through a closing."

"I have to go."

****

When Declan came back from getting coffee, he announced that Luke had left to go back to the hotel. Skylar was ready to strangle her brother. Even with the assurance he'd taken a uniform with him, it still left her uneasy. The only thing that kept her mind from worry was helping Olivia room hop after being kicked out of the first assigned room and having to move next door. After leaving them alone with a uniform in the room, her brother disappeared, saying he'd be back later to check on them. Skylar helped Olivia into the bed. She pulled the covers up over Olivia's legs.

"I'm not an invalid, Sky."

"Shut up and let me baby you." She grinned.

"Bite me." Olivia smiled.

"Aw, now there's my smartass best friend...she's still in there."

Olivia chuckled. "You wouldn't love me any other way."

"Two peas in a pod as my brothers used to call us." Skylar walked over to the water jug and shook it. "You're on E. I'm going for a refill."

"Sky, that's not a good idea."

The officer moved to block the door. "I'm afraid I can't let you do that, ma'am."

"Henry, my name isn't ma'am." Skyler pulled her revolver out of her jeans and showed Henry. "I'll be fine. I'm going right down the hall for a refill. I'll scream and shoot if anything happens to me, and not necessarily in that order."

Henry's lips twitched. "You're going to get me fired, Skylar."

"Nah, it can be our secret."

She gently shoved Henry out of the way. "I'll be back in a few minutes. What's going to happen? If I know my brother, he's got cops all throughout the building, and we're on the fifth floor."

He frowned but didn't stop her from leaving. "I'm timing you."

She grinned and opened the door, whistling her way down the empty corridor into the break room. She moved to the ice machine and shoved the container beneath it. The cubes in the machine crunched as they fell into the oversized thermos.

"Don't be stupid," a man whispered in her ear while shoving his gun in her side. The thermos in her hand dropped to the floor, and ice skittered across the linoleum. His hands made quick work over her body before pulling the gun hidden in her waistband. He jabbed his gun back in her side. "You make a sound, I'll shoot you, and then I'll come back and shoot the cop and the girl hiding in the room."

"Why are you doing this?"

He shoved the gun in her side harder. "I said not a sound."

She chewed her lip as she let him lead her out the security exit, knowing this might be the last few moments of her life. She tripped on the stairs as he rushed her down the flights and continued into the underground parking garage, shoving her out through the exit. When the door clicked closed behind her, she swallowed around her apprehension.

"Why are you doing this? I don't even know you."

"Shut up," he said louder as she struggled from his grasp.

****

"Boss, she went for water two minutes ago and isn't back."

"I know," Declan huffed into the phone as he jumped down the stairs two at a time. "He's headed for the parking garage. I'm two flights behind them. Send backup."

****

Luke parked in the doctors' lot, closest to the door and got out, heading for the door when it burst open. He ducked behind a concrete column and peered around the edge to find Skylar with the guy from the bar. Her demand for answers was visibly making her assailant pissed. The exit door kicked open again, and Declan eased out with the gun pointed at the pair.

"Drop the weapon, asshole."

The man grabbed Skylar around the neck and held the gun to her head. "I don't think so, pig. One wrong move and she gets a bullet to the brain." He cocked the trigger.

She pulled on his arm, fighting a losing battle in trying to get free.

"Shoot the asshole."

Declan moved the gun looking for the right angle. "I don't have a shot."

"God damn it, Dec, shoot this son of bitch. If I'm dying, he's going with me."

His hold on her throat tightened. "Shut up," he growled in her ear.

Luke inched out from behind the column and approached them from the rear. Declan's eyes darted to him and back to Sky's.

"Skylar, listen very carefully."

Tears streaked down her red face as she gasped for air in the man's hold.

"Remember when I stole your precious doll and threatened to tear her head off? You remember what you did to Flynn when he was restraining you?"

She double blinked.

"It's that time again."

She stepped to the side, her fist coming down hard on the assailant's crotch. When he doubled over, he lost his hold, and she elbowed him in the nose and scurried out of his reach.

Luke jumped on top of her, sending

them both to the concrete ground, covering her body with his.

Two gun shots rang out through the concrete garage as she struggled from beneath Luke's hold to see if her assailant was hit. He lay dead on the ground with a bullet hole between his eyes. Blood seeped beneath his head. She glanced over at Declan. He was lying on the ground, holding his hand to his chest.

"Dec..." Luke called out, jumping up and hurrying over to Declan's side. He tore his shirt open and peeled the layers back. "Shit. Sky, call for medics."

A team of police officers burst through the door. The lead uniform keyed the mic. "Love's been hit. Send the paramedics into the parking garage."

Luke used his hand to press on the wound, trying to staunch the flow of blood as a gurney was wheeled out. The paramedics moved everyone out of the way and slid Declan on before whisking him away again.

She stood beside Luke and watched her brother being carted away while another team, and the officers left behind, dealt with the dead guy. In a trance, Luke stared down at the blood on his hands.

"Sky, you need to call your parents."

Sky led him into the hospital and up the stairs into one of the ladies restrooms, not carrying if it was occupied. She held his hands under the water and soaped her hands and helped him wash the fresh blood away. The warm water snapped him out of his daze and he finished his hands alone, drying them before cupping her face and pressing his lips to hers in a punishing kiss.

"He almost killed you."

"But he didn't, Luke. He didn't hurt me. Besides, I knew Henry would tell on me if I wasn't back in two minutes. I was counting on it."

He leaned his forehead against hers. "It's over." The words were a whisper between them.

"He never told me why he did it." She pressed a kiss to his lips before pulling out her phone and dialing her parents.

"I'm sure it's just a matter of time until the police put the pieces together."

Skylar held up her finger. "Mom. Declan was shot saving my life. I need Dad and you to come to the hospital."

"Martin, grab your keys," her mother yelled. "We have to go. Baby, are you okay? Are you hurt?"

"Just scratched up, but I'm fine. I've got to go find where they took him."

"We'll be there in ten minutes. Hold tight, honey. Momma's coming."

Tears gathered in Skylar's eyes. "Thanks, Mom. I love you."

"I love you too, baby."

A single tear fell, and Luke pulled her into his arms, holding her while her shoulders shook. Her mind raced, replaying the incident and seeing Declan so hurt.

"It's okay, Sky. Let it out. I've got you."

She sniffled and broke his hold, wiping her tear-stained face. "Not until I know about Declan. When I know he's going to be okay, then I'll have my breakdown."

Luke kissed her forehead and led her out of the bathroom to the uniform that had apparently followed them.

"They took him straight to surgery on the fourth floor."

"Thank you," she whispered.

Luke took her hand and squeezed it as they made their way to the fourth floor, where several cops sat in the surgical waiting room. Olivia sat alone in a set of chairs.

"What are you doing out of bed?"

"Like they could keep me still, please." She gestured to Henry. "Henry here heard it all over the radio. I threatened to castrate him if he didn't take me to the waiting room."

She rose. "Are you okay?" Olivia took Skylar's arms and turned them. "Did you get shot? Did he hurt you?"

"No, just a few scratches." She turned back to the door. "Have they come out and said anything?"

"No. I tried to call your parents, but no one answered."

"That's because I already called them. They're on their way."

Declan's second-in-command, Deputy Chief Simmons, approached them. "Ms. Love, if there's anything you need, we're here for you."

"Thank you."

"Baby," Skylar's mom called, rushing into the waiting room with open arms. Skylar was engulfed and surrounded by the love of her mother as her dad stood watch. Her mother squeezed her tight and kissed her cheek. "Are you all right? Have you heard anything? Do I need to go find the doctor for answers?"

"No, Mom, Declan's in surgery, and it probably wouldn't be good if you tried to break in demanding answers. As for me, I'm fine. A psycho tried to abduct me; Declan and Luke saved me."

Her mother's gaze shot to Luke. "You saved my baby?"

"No, ma'am. She pretty much saved herself, giving Declan an opening to shoot the bast....I mean, psycho. I just covered her during the gunfight."

"You saved my baby." She ignored Luke's explanation and threw her arms around him. "I always knew you were a good boy."

Skylar tried to hide her smile,

watching as Luke was engulfed in an awkward hug.

He patted her back. "Honestly....It was all Declan..."

"No." She finally let go. "Stray bullets are a real thing, and you put your life in front of hers."

"Sky, how you holding up?" her dad asked, putting his arm around her shoulders.

"I'll be better when we hear news on Declan."

Her father led her over to one of the chairs and sat next to Olivia and her. "Okay, girls, start talking. Olivia, you can start with why in the hell you're pulling around an IV bag."

"Sky's psycho hit me on the back of the head before he burned down our shop."

Sky's father rested his elbows on his legs. "That's what happened? We heard there was a fire but we didn't think it was your shop."

He glanced at Sky. "Your turn."

She spent thirty minutes getting her parents caught up with everything that had happened since Friday night, leaving out all the juicy details of what had happened between Luke and her. About the time she finished, her brothers showed up and she had to repeat the story.

9 CHAPTER

Sky glanced up from her slouched positon to see the doctor pulling off his mask as he approached the waiting room. She stood, placing a trembling hand on her stomach. Luke wrapped his arm around her waist and pulled her close.

"Mrs. Love?"

"Yes." Her mom stood up, her father's reassuring hand on her back.

"Surgery went well. The bullet went straight through and he only suffered minor damage. He's in recovery and still groggy from the anesthesia, but when he wakes up, we're moving him into a room, and we'll come back to get you.

Her father shook the doctor's hand. "Thank you, Doctor."

Luke pressed a kiss to Skylar's forehead. Out of the corner of her eye, she saw her father take notice.

"How about I go get us some coffee?" Luke whispered in her ear. "After we visit with Declan, I'm going to take you home and get you cleaned up."

He lifted her arm and turned it, observing her scratches. The same scratches she had forgotten were there.

"Come on, Olivia. It's time to go back to your room."

Olivia rose and glared at her warden. "Didn't you hear? The bad guy's dead. I won't be needing your services."

"Until Declan tells me otherwise, I'm afraid you're stuck with me," Henry reminded her.

"Remind me to kill your brother when he wakes up," she whispered to Sky in passing. "Call me later."

"I will." Sky squeezed Olivia's hand as she walked out. "Thanks for being here."

She smirked at Henry. "I wouldn't have had it any other way."

"And she means that, Ms. Love," Henry chimed in.

Forty minutes and two cups of coffee later, a nurse came in to escort them to Declan's room. Most of the officers, that had shown, had left with the message to let Declan know that they'd be back to visit. Deputy Chief Simmons announced he'd be back later tonight to talk to Declan and that he would go check the dead guy's background to see if he could pinpoint any connection between the dead man, Luke and her. She'd wished him luck.

Declan was resting comfortably when they entered, alert and aggravated that the nurse kept having to remind him he couldn't just get up and move.

"There's my baby boy." Her mom started across the room, leaning over the bed and peppering him with tiny kisses all over his face.

"Mom, quit. I'm not a baby."

"You'll always be my baby," she quickly replied while straightening the blanket on the bed and making sure he was covered.

Declan rolled his eyes. "Thanks, mom." He glanced at Sky. "You okay?"

"Yeah." She waved off his concern. "Thank god you stole my baby doll when I was young." She grinned. "Or I might not have been."

He chuckled and then clutched his chest and coughed. "Good thing we toughened you up. If you'd been a girly girl, we'd all be hurt because I wasn't letting him take you. Maybe next time you'll listen and stay put when you're told."

"Keep kidding yourself, Dec." Luke chuckled.

Sky moved beside the bed and squeezed Declan's hand. "I'm so sorry, Declan. It's all my fault." Her eyes glassed over.

"Now don't go blaming yourself, Sky. He was probably crazy long before he met you. I'm just glad you're okay. Did you recognize him from anywhere besides the restaurant?"

"No, and I asked him why he was doing this, but he never gave me an answer."

Declan's brows dipped. "Is Simmons looking for a connection?"

She nodded and swiped away the tear that slipped free.

"I'm sure he'll find it," he reassured her. "He's like a hound dog sniffing out a bone. You look like hell. Why don't you go home and get some rest? It doesn't look like I'll be going anywhere." She didn't miss the look that Declan gave Luke or the slight nod of his head toward the door.

"Come on, Sky. I'm going to take you home." He rested his palm on her lower back. "I'll come back tomorrow to visit. If you need anything, call me."

Skylar hugged her parents one last time before following Luke out of the room. Her shoulders sagged, as did her heart. She was ready to drop on her feet. She followed Luke into the parking garage and out the door. Two wet spots remained where the blood had been washed away. Her heart clenched.

"It's over." Luke slid his fingers through hers.

She gave a slight nod and swallowed around the lump in her throat before getting into his SUV. She slid the buckle in place and rested her head. She fought to reassure her mind, even if she couldn't make sense of any of it. The facts were the man was dead and her brother lay in a hospital bed.

****

Luke drove straight to the cabin, taking the long way and purposely avoiding her boutique. That was added stress that could wait one more day. Her strong veneer was cracking, and if she had a breakdown, he'd help her through it. A quick look from the corner of his eye and he noticed her dazed expression. The only noise was the hum coming from the air conditioner vents. She needed a jolt to get out of her head, something to counteract the miserable day.

He pulled into the drive, parked the car, and pulled the keys. "Sky?"

"Hmm?" she answered, unmoving, her gaze out the front window.

"Marry me."

"What?" She blinked several time

before whipping her gaze to his. "You're nuts."

He shrugged. "That's not quite the response I was looking for. A yes or no would have sufficed."

She unbuckled her belt and shifted in her seat. "What did you expect? We've been almost poisoned. Everything I've worked for has just gone up into flames; I was kidnapped; Declan was shot, and now you go and pull this? A marriage proposal? Luke, we've been running on adrenaline." She took a deep breath, opened the door, and slid out heading for the porch.

"And...she's back." He grinned and slid out of the car, before following her into the cabin. "Sky, you didn't answer my question."

She was heading for the hallway, but his comment had her stopping dead in her tracks. She slowly turned to face him. "I would have given you an answer had you meant it. I know what you just did. It was like a splash of cold water to my face. I needed it. So, thank you."

"And what would have been your answer if I'd 'meant it'?" He made quotation marks in the air.

"It doesn't matter, Luke." She shrugged. "It wasn't real." She spun on her heels and disappeared down the hallway.

"What if it was?" he whispered to himself.

"I heard that," she hollered back at him. "No more talk of marriage tonight or anything else."

He grinned and walked to the fridge. After grabbing a beer and popping the top, he leaned his hip against the counter as he took a long pull of the icy brew.

Minutes later, she appeared in the hallway with a towel wrapped around her body. His cock grew thicker every second he stared at the perfection he knew was hidden beneath. He swallowed, his beer forgotten. "You need me to wash your back?"

"Not quite." She tossed him his swim trunks and another towel. "But you can join me for a relaxing dip in the hot springs."

"You don't have to ask me twice." He stripped in front of her and changed, and they were out the door minutes later. "I figured you'd be tired and need sleep."

"You thought wrong." She walked down the short path to their destination. "Believe it or not, my brother doesn't know what I need." She let the towel fall to her feet, standing naked before him. "But I'm betting you do."

She smiled and eased into the water.

"Damn right I do, woman." He hopped to get out of his swim trunks, dropped them on the towel, and followed her in. His cock jetted out in front of him, as if to reach her first. He eased under the water and pulled her into his arms, holding her while pressing his back into the rocks. His hands rested at her waist when she wrapped her legs around him. He held her still, letting her feel the length of his shaft as it rubbed against her wet folds. Steam rose around them. The warm water eased his tired muscles.

He pressed his lips to her collarbone, working a slow, agonizing path up her neck. "I guess you've decided it's play time?" he asked between kisses until reaching her lips. He took them in a deep kiss, taking his time and claiming every inch of her mouth until she pressed closer to his body. He reached between their bodies and slid his fingers against her folds before sliding them in.

He swallowed her moan before adding another, working them in and out.

She broke the kiss and reached for his shaft, stroking him from the base to the tip.

"You fight dirty, Sky."

She grinned. "You don't even know what I'm capable of."

He pulled his fingers free, positioned her over his cock, and eased her down his length. "I can't wait to find out."

He lifted her weightless body up,

sliding her up and down his shaft, working her into a state of frenzy while trying to contain himself. "I think we may have to borrow Declan's handcuffs one night. Would you like that, Sky?"

She moaned. Her nails dug deeper into his back.

"I'll take that as a yes."

"I don't need his. I have my own."

Damn. Her words made his cock throb against her silky folds. He quickened their pace, watching her breasts as they bounced in the water. He wasn't going to last, and damn, if she wasn't coming with him.

He eased one hand between them and found her clit as she used her legs to continue the motion. He circled the tiny nub, using his thumb to add pressure.

"Oh god," she called out.

Her channel tightened around him, squeezing him as her orgasm hit. His name was a moan on her lips as he stilled inside her, fully seating himself inside of her to the hilt, shooting his seed to soak her womb.

Her racing heart matched his as their chests rose and fell in quick succession, each vying to breathe.

Silence lingered between them as he held her gaze. Words were left unspoken. He loved her, yet she wasn't ready to hear it. Not like this, not here and now. He swallowed around his dry throat and kissed her, trying as he might to convey his feelings through his gentle kiss.

He rested his head against the rock. "Wow."

She slid off him, taking the warmth of her body.

"You can say that again." She chuckled. "You knew exactly what I needed." Skylar rested her back next to his and looked up at the night sky. "So what happens now?"

He glanced at her. "I guess dating like normal people."

She smiled. "Luke, we'll never be normal."

He pushed off the rock and moved in front of her, his hands on her hips. "That's what I love about you, about us. I can be myself with you. No more pretending that I'm something I'm not."

She rested her hand on his cheek. "I've always known who you are. You're a good man, Luke Tanner." She pressed her palm to his chest. "In here."

His heart skipped a beat. "You take my breath away, Sky. All of this wasted time..."

"It wasn't wasted, Luke. Finding cures is what you were meant to do. It makes you who you are." Her eyes searched his, and he could see the love in her eyes without the words.

He held her gaze. "I can't lose you." *I love you.*

She visibly swallowed. "You won't."

He kissed her as if she held a direct line to his heart. Fighting to hold back his words was one of the hardest things he'd had to endure.

****

Sky lay naked under the covers. The morning light seeped through the curtains warming her face as she snuggled in Luke's arms. After the hot springs, they'd come back and made love again, and she fell asleep as he held her. He was the only part of her world that was right. Her mind drifted to the store, and the headaches that would wait for her until she rejoined the real world. Her life on the run was coming to an end. She closed her eyes, wanting to savor the feel of his body, afraid if she got up then everything would change.

"I can hear the wheels turning." Luke kissed her forehead. His fingers drew a lazy path over her arm. "Whatcha thinking about?"

"Everything I've got to do today." She leaned up and rested her weight on her elbow. "If you're moving back, where are you going to stay? Have you found a house?"

"Not yet." He smiled. "I was hoping you'd help me pick one out."

She rested her head against his chest, her palm over his heart. "You can stay with me while you look."

He rolled on top of her, settling between her thighs. "You mean you're not making me sleep on the streets?"

She rolled her eyes and giggled as he nudged closer to her heat. "You're a millionaire. You could easily renovate the top floor of the Dagger building into a sweet bachelor pad."

He chuckled as he placed lazy kisses on her chest. "Is that what I am? A bachelor?"

She wrapped her legs around him, lifted her hips, and used her hold to slide his shaft into her. "No...you're taken."

"Damn right I am."

She spent the next hour reminding him just how taken he was before reminding him again in the shower.

They both dressed and ate breakfast before he drove her back to her place. He pulled up in the driveway and let the car idle. "I'm going to go take care of some business and then check on Declan. What are your plans?"

"I'm going to deal with the store." She let out a long sigh. "And check on Olivia. Do you want to meet for lunch?"

His lips twitched. "Absolutely, only this

time I pick the place. How about Channing's at noon?"

She chuckled before kissing him and getting out of the car. She took a quick glance at her watch. "Absolutely."

She closed the door and watched him until he turned off her road before spinning on her heels and hefting her bag over her shoulder.

She dropped her keys on the table in the foyer and carried her bag straight to the laundry room. The stillness in her house was an unfamiliar feeling after the week she'd had. She opened her windows to let the fresh air in on the breeze while whisking the stale air out. The smell of the clean, salty air drifted to her nose, renewing her spirit and rejuvenating her strength.

She called the fire inspector to hear they'd determined an accelerant had been used, but they were still determining the origin. Did it matter where it started? She already knew who'd started it. What she still didn't understand was why. Regardless, the building was off-limits while they investigated, so she was at a standstill on repairing any of the damage.

She spent the early afternoon making the rest of her calls, to Declan, her insurance agent, and the police station to see if they'd found the connection, dealing with all of the things that might offer her some closure. She wanted to forget everything that had happened, to pretend that life was normal. Only her brain wasn't cooperating. She kept going over each of the incidents, unable to put her finger on a specific reason that could have started the snowball effect in her life.

She checked her watch and hurried to close the house. She was ten minutes late for their lunch date.

10 CHAPTER

Luke strolled into the hotel to find Justin reading the paper and drinking a cup of coffee in the lobby.

He closed the paper, folded it beneath his arm, and picked up his coffee. "Luke, I've been trying to call you all morning."

Luke pulled out his phone and glanced at the black screen. "Sorry, it's dead." He'd turned to walk toward the elevator when Justin stopped him and turned him around to face the front door. "You've got a closing on the mainland, and you're about to miss the ferry. Megan Dagger won't sign unless she meets you in person."

"But I was supposed to meet Sky at Channing's for lunch."

"I'll meet her and explain why you

couldn't make it. If I'm going to be living here, I might as well get to know the locals." Justin shoved his cell phone into Luke's hand.

"Megan's number is in my phone, and the GPS is loaded with the directions to the closing agent. Now go. She'll never sell it to you if she thinks you stood her up."

"You'll meet Sky?"

"Of course."

"She's important to me."

"I got it. I'll be on my best behavior. Now go."

Luke jogged back to his SUV and hopped inside, dialing Sky from Justin's phone. She didn't answer. "Shit." He shoved Justin's phone into his pocket and plugged his into the car charger before pulling out and heading toward the ferry. He'd have to make it up to Skylar with a celebration dinner and see Declan when he got back.

****

Declan smiled as Olivia entered the hospital room with Henry on her heels. "Miss me already?"

"Puhlease." She rolled her eyes. "What kind of a best friend would I be to Sky if I didn't make sure you weren't scaring away the doctors? Besides, you're the only one that can call off the dog." She gestured toward Henry. "No offense."

"None taken."

Declan gave the nod of approval and waited until Henry left. "You feeling better?"

"Oh yeah, you know it takes a lot more than a blow to the back of my head to take me out of the game. How are you feeling?"

She moved to sit on the side of his bed. "I've had better days," he admitted.

She moved to the window avoiding eye contact with him.

He cleared his throat. "So why are you still here? I called the guard off."

She spun to meet his smiling face.

"Jerk. I just thought you might like some company."

Instantly, he knew she was lying, thanks to his gift, but he bit his tongue, not calling her out.

The door flew open, and Simmons walked in with a file in his hand. "I've got something."

Olivia moved closer but stood just out of reach.

"Jerry Mitchell."

"Who?"

"The guy who shot you," he reminded Declan. "I couldn't find a tie directly to Skylar or Olivia, but I did find this."

He pulled out a bank statement and handed it to Declan. "Three transactions of ten thousand dollars, all starting the day Luke came on the island."

Declan scanned the paper and verified the dates. "From who? Amanda?"

"No, that's the kicker. Justin Healy."

Declan's gaze shot up. "That's Luke's assistant. He's here on the island. Send a unit to watch Skylar and alert Luke, and then put out an APB on this son of a bitch."

"I already did," he answered. "Skylar isn't home. We're still trying to locate her."

Declan winced as he tried to get out of the bed. Olivia laid her hand on his shoulder and eased him back into the mattress. "You can't go."

"We'll find them."

"Check with the fire inspector. She was probably dealing with that today."

"We'll keep you posted," Simmons called out as he hurried from the room.

Olivia picked up the hospital phone and tried Sky's cell. It went to voicemail.

"Sky, this is Olivia. Justin is behind this. Tell Luke and go to the police or somewhere safe until they catch him."

****

Luke pulled up at the ferry to find it would be delayed thirty minutes. He pulled out Justin's phone and scrolled through to look for Megan's number. He paused on Amanda's name at the top of the list. His brows dipped. "What the…"

He continued down to Megan and dialed.

"Hello."

"Ms. Dagger. This is Luke Tanner, and I'm just calling to let you know that I'm delayed getting to the signing."

"Mr. Tanner? I've already signed two days ago. Didn't your assistant tell you?"

"No. I'm sorry. I'll reschedule for tomorrow if that's okay."

"Sure," she agreed. "I'm just happy to get rid of that old building."

"Thanks." Luke hung up and went straight into Justin's text messages and opened the ones between Amanda and him. His stomach dropped into his feet as he read the explicit details about their relationship and how Justin would rather see Luke dead than to play the charade any longer.

"Fuck…"

He got out of the messages and called the hospital as he hurried to get in his car. Olivia answered Declan's phone and put him right on.

"Justin orchestrated the whole thing."

"I know. We just found it in his bank records. Tell me that Sky is with you. We can't find her."

Luke gripped the steering wheel tighter and clenched his teeth. "Justin is meeting her for lunch at Channing's at noon. He claimed I had a closing on the Dagger building, and I was late, so he went in my place."

"Shit, God damn it. If that motherfucker touches her..."

"Call your guys. I'm on the way."

****

"Skylar?"

She spun around. "Yes?"

A man extended his hand. The energy around him was a pukey yellow. "I'm Justin, Luke's assistant. I'm afraid he's been called away and won't be able to make it to lunch."

Skylar gave him a sad smile. "That's okay. I'm sure it was important."

"If you'd like to eat with me, I'm starving."

"No, that's okay. I've got some things to take care of today anyway."

She turned and headed back to her car, listening to her voicemail as she went to shove the key inside.

She heard Olivia's panicked voice. "Justin is behind everything. Get somewhere safe."

Her heart raced, and as she tried to open the door, she felt the bite of steel in her side. She didn't need to look over her shoulder to know who held the gun. He slipped her phone out of her fingers and dropped it to the ground, crushing it with his foot.

He took her keys and kept the gun pointed at her. "Get in the car."

She slowly got in the driver's side as he rounded the car and got in the other side. She buckled her belt as he shoved the keys into the ignition.

"Where are you taking me?"

"The Dagger building," he announced, turning in his seat to face her, ignoring his seatbelt.

She'd bit her tongue to stop from telling him to buckle up. What did she care if the asshole was in a crash?

"You've ruined everything. If Luke had stayed with Amanda, I wouldn't be on this piece-of-shit little island, and I'd be rich."

Apprehension filled Skylar's gut as she eased out onto the road. The gun in his right hand pointed at her side.

"I had nothing to do with Luke leaving Amanda. He knew she was cheating on him."

"I know." His lips turned up in an evil grin. "With me. But if it hadn't been for you, he wouldn't have wanted to move back to this godforsaken place. This date is special; she's important; blah blah blah... He made my ears bleed."

"Why'd you kill Amanda if you loved her?"

"I didn't kill her." He gawked. "That

KATE ALLENTON

fuckhead killed her when I refused to pay
him his last payment after he botched the
drinks."

"Luke's going to come for me, along
with the entire police department. They've
tied you to the guy from the hospital.
There's nowhere you can hide on the
island where they won't find you."

"He's not coming for you, sweetheart."
He chuckled. "He's on a ferry going to a
closing that already took place, on the
same building where you're going to die."
He huffed. "It's fitting really. He's going to
own it, and you died there. A constant
reminder of what he's done."

She had only four miles before she got
to the building. She was running out of
time if she was going to make it out of this
alive. Her eyes scanned the car as sweat
beaded on her brow. There was no way
she was walking into that building. If she
died, it wouldn't be there.

She spotted her opportunity and
clutched the wheel with both hands,
pressing down on the accelerator.

"What are you doing?" he asked. "Slow
down or I'll shoot."

"You won't shoot. Then you'll die, too,
when the car crashes." She gritted her
teeth and pressed harder, trying to keep
control as she veered the car off the road.
It bumped and jolted as she hit the
shoulder and grass before ramming the

passenger side into a large pine tree. His airbag exploded, smashing his face. She heard the crack from the bones in his nose before blood gushed out. She winced as she scrambled to get her seatbelt off. His fingers still clutched the gun. Cupping his nose, he sneered at her. The black and blue around his eyes already started to show. He raised the gun as she jumped out, taking cover by the rear door.

"I'll fucking kill you," he screamed out.

She limped into the woods, ignoring the pain that radiated through her entire body. She held her neck to help ease what felt like thousands of pins prickling her neck and collarbone. If he was going to kill her, the fucker had to catch her first, and she had a good head start since he was wedged in because of the tree. He'd have to climb out the other side of the car and that gave her the head start she needed.

She'd dragged herself far into the woods when she realized where she was. "The camping grounds," she whispered to herself, easing over the fallen tree in her path. Her breath came out in pants. Anything bigger and her lungs protested with coughing and wheezing.

She couldn't stop; she wouldn't stop. A city boy from New York was no match for a local on this island. She heard his scream from behind her, just as she found the camping grounds empty, and realized he was probably free.

She hurried around. Her eyes darted around each corner for a weapon, anything that one of the local explorers might have left behind, and that's when she spotted the broken tent drifting on the breeze from the makeshift camp left behind. Cut-up firewood and empty food cans. She dropped to her knees, measuring each item as a potential weapon. Moving the firewood to her side, she spotted the glass bottle. She cracked it against a tree and held the three pieces of broken glass in her hand.

She ripped the sleeve off her shirt and used it to clutch the makeshift knife and save her fingers. When she heard him, she held her weapon, pressing her back into the bark of an oak tree while waiting for him to find her. Her heart raced and her hands shook. Her heartbeat thumped loudly in her ears.

She heard the crackle of leaves as he approached further into the camping area and then stopped.

"Justin," Luke called out. "You don't want her. You want me. Well, here I am. You want to fight? Then drop the gun and fight me like a man, instead of going after a woman like the coward you are."

She peeked around the tree to find Luke holding his hands open wide.

Justin leveled the gun using his bloody

hand to aim the gun at Luke.

She eased out of her hiding spot, taking measured steps so he wouldn't hear her approach from behind.

Luke spotted her and his eyes widened for a split second before he kept taunting Luke, probably to cover her sounds.

"If you didn't want to live here, you should have just quit."

"You're so fucking stupid," Justin spat out. "You ruined everything. Why couldn't you just stay with Amanda? All of this could have been prevented."

Luke held up Justin's phone. "I read your text conversations with her. She was playing you just like she did me. You were just too blind to see it."

Skylar plunged the glass into Justin's back, twisting it as the gun fired. Luke dove for the ground as Skylar pulled the weapon out and plunged it in again. Justin dropped to his knees; the gun fell from his hand, and she scurried to pick it up. In the distance, sirens wailed, and she knew that the cavalry was on the way, even if they were too late. Justin fell to his side and his eyes closed as blood seeped from his wounds.

Luke jumped up and hurried to her side, easing the gun from her hands. He tossed it behind them and pulled her into his arms.

Her shoulders shook as realization of

what she'd just done hit her like a ton of bricks. "I killed him," she cried and clutched Luke's shirt.

"Shhh....It was either him or us, baby." He smoothed her hair and bent down to eye level. "You saved my life." He pulled her to his chest again as the tears fell.

"I told him you would come," she said through her sobs. "He didn't believe me."

Luke stroked her back. "I'll always come for you, always." He broke his embrace and looked her in the eyes. "You're my heart, Sky. I'll never give up on you, or us. I love you."

Their moment was lost when the police, trampling through the woods, spotted them; Simmons was leading the charge.

"Are you okay?" he asked. "I saw the car."

"I think I bruised my lungs on impact and have whiplash. My entire body aches."

"We need to get you checked out."

"Simmons," one of the officers called out. His fingers pressed to Justin's neck. "He's breathing. We need paramedics."

Simmons used the radio attached to his lapel to have the medical team, which apparently was on route, hurry through the woods to their location.

When they arrived, one crew went to Justin while another ordered her onto a stretcher. Luke walked beside her as she was carried out. He rode with her to the hospital and stayed with her while they admitted her and then as she waited for x-rays to be done. She'd suffered a broken rib. Her bruised midsection had already turned black and blue before they ever turned the x-ray machine on. They ordered her a room for observation and that's when Luke pulled the doctor aside and talked in hushed tones.

"Fine, but only for a few minutes. She'll be in the room next door."

Luke helped ease her into the wheelchair and pushed her from the room. "Where are we going?"

"There's someone who needs to see that you're okay, or he'll kill both of us. I hear he's already causing quite a stir and the nurses can't keep him contained."

"Declan." She smiled.

He rolled her onto the elevator, up to Declan's floor, and inside his room.

His yanking on his IV stilled as he held her gaze. "I was just coming to find you."

"No need." She gave him a sad smile. "So lie back down before you get us both in trouble."

11 CHAPTER

One month later, Skylar and Olivia stood on the sidewalk watching as the bricklayers added each brick to her new building. "What do you think of that one?"

"He has a nice body." Olivia tilted her head. "But I don't think so."

"You've said that about all of the ones I've picked out for you. So just tell me which one you think is the cream of the crop."

Oliva bit her nails as she eyed the shirtless construction guys, never answering Sky's question.

A police siren blared behind them and they glanced over their shoulders to find Declan getting out of the car and walking over to them.

"He's the one." Olivia pointed to one of the construction guys carrying wood over his shoulder.

"He's the one what?" Declan asked.

"He's the one she thinks is the hottest," Sky chimed in, holding back her grin.

"Sky, you have a boyfriend," he announced.

She shrugged. "I didn't pick him."

Olivia chuckled. "No, you picked *him*." And she pointed to one of the other guys.

Skylar's mouth parted. "Not for me, for you."

"You're late for Sunday dinner. Do you need a lift?"

"I'm taking her," Olivia answered, never taking her gaze from the good-looking man now staring at her and grinning from ear to ear. She wiggled her fingers and giggled.

"Fine," Declan growled. "But I'm not saving you any damn dessert if you don't hurry your asses up."

Skylar nudged Olivia. "He's getting cranky in his old age."

They glanced back to watch him leave before heading for the car. "He's just jealous."

"Sky, he isn't interested in me. He only tolerates me because I'm your best friend."

The drive to Skylar's parents' house

was short. They could have walked the distance, but in the blazing sun, they didn't want to arrive all sweaty.

"How's it going with Luke?"

Skylar grinned. Since leaving the hospital, things between them had changed. He'd been staying with her when he wasn't back in New York getting the employees and part of his company ready to move. "He picked out a house."

"So it's official." Olivia's eyes lit up. "He's here for good."

"Looks that way." Skylar could barely contain her excitement.

"Oh, I'm so happy for you." Olivia reached over and squeezed Skylar's arm. "You deserve it. You both do."

"We're just dating, Olivia, and it's only been a month."

Olivia parked the car behind all of the SUVs that lined the road in front of Skylar's parents' house. "Who's missing today?"

Skylar let out a long sigh. "Landon. I swear I'm going to have to go track that little shit down and drag him home to see Mom. He's breaking her heart."

They got out of the car and headed toward the sound of her mother's favorite music.

She gasped as she rounded the corner. The entire backyard was surrounded in Skylar's favorite flowers. Luke stood in the middle of the yard, wearing a suit. Everyone was watching her.

Olivia grasped her arm. "Oh my god," she whispered. "Sky..."

Skylar walked slowly into the yard, her gaze going over her brothers and landing on her father with his arm around her mother's shoulder. Her mom's eyes were filled with tears.

She stopped in front of Luke and glanced once more over her shoulder at her family before turning to address him.

"What are you doing, and why are you dressed like that?" she whispered.

He smiled. The energy around him shifted to an amazing shade of light blue. "I wanted them to witness this."

"Luke..." Her eyes widened.

He took her hands in his. "Skylar Love. I've known you my entire life. You're the reason I breathe, the reason I look forward to getting up in the mornings. I didn't know what true happiness and love were until I came back to the island, to you, and I never want to let that go. I'll love you forever and always." He pulled out a box from his pocket and opened it. "Please, do me the honor of becoming my wife."

Her heart raced as she glanced down at the ring and then up into his eyes. She nodded as tears welled behind her eyes. "Yes."

Cheers sounded from behind them as

he took the ring out and slid it on her finger.

"I love you," she whispered as his lips closed the distance between them. "God, I love you."

He kissed her, tilting her over his arm, and she opened her eyes to find the color surrounding Luke and her had turned to the light pink like that of her parents. She laughed as he straightened them both and turned to her family.

"She said yes," he shouted, and they were both engulfed in arms and congratulations.

"We get to plan a wedding." Olivia did a little happy dance.

"And you get to walk with Declan," Skylar announced, doing her own version of the dance.

Olivia's smile fell and her body froze.

"Still, we get to plan a wedding," she said again, ignoring Sky's comment.

"It will have to wait until after the champagne," Sky's father announced.

The entire group headed inside, leaving Luke and her alone in the backyard. She took his hands. "Are you sure you want to do this?"

"I've never been more sure of anything in my life. Skylar, I love you. I'm ready to scream it from the rooftops. I can't imagine living another day without you in my life."

She laced her fingers behind his neck. "I knew one day my dream would become a reality."

He tossed his head back and laughed. "You're going to keep me on my toes, aren't you?"

"You can count on it." She smiled bigger.

"Any other plans you've dreamt of that I should know about?"

"Children," she answered. "But they can wait a few years." She pressed her lips to his in a kiss between lovers before wrapping her hand around his bicep and walking toward the house. "You're going to be a great dad."

The End

ABOUT THE AUTHOR

Kate has lived in Florida for most of her entire life. She enjoys a quiet life with her husband, Michael and two kids.

Kate has pulled all-nighters finishing her favorite books and also writing them. She says she'll sleep when she's dead or when her muse stops singing off key.

She loves creating worlds full of suspense, secrets, hunky men, kick ass heroines, steamy sex and oh yeah the love of a lifetime. Not to mention an occasional ghost and other supernatural talents thrown into the mix.